THE HORROR

Look out for all the books in
THE HOUSE ON CHERRY STREET
trilogy:

Point

THE HOUSE ON CHERRY STREET

BOOK 2: THE HORROR

**Rodman Philbrick
and Lynn Harnett**

■SCHOLASTIC

Scholastic Children's Books,
Commonwealth House, 1-19 New Oxford Street,
London WC1A 1NU, UK
a division of Scholastic Ltd
London ~ New York ~ Toronto ~ Sydney ~ Auckland

First published in the US by Scholastic Inc, 1995
This edition published in the UK by Scholastic Ltd, 1997

ISBN 0 590 13886 3

Printed by Cox and Wyman Ltd, Reading, Berks.

10 9 8 7 6 5 4 3 2 1

For Gillian, Nate, Ian, Kate and Cassie

THE HORROR

1

The baby-sitter didn't believe in ghosts.

"Don't be silly," she said. "There's no such thing as a haunted house."

Her name was Katie, and she was a teenager with red hair and an attitude — meaning she thought I was a total dweeb for trying to tell her about the ghosts in the house on Cherry Street.

"Don't say I didn't warn you," I said stubbornly.

She smirked at me and then shaded her eyes, looking up at the decaying mansion my family had rented for the summer. "What a place!" she said. "It really is kind of spooky looking."

My parents didn't believe in ghosts, either, and they'd left Katie in charge while they went away on a business trip. Not that I needed a baby-sitter or anything. At twelve I can pretty much look after myself. But my little sister Sally was only four and the ghosts were *very* interested in her.

1

"I better go inside," Katie announced cheerfully. "Check things out."

And then she marched up the steps and walked right through the door of that creepy old house as if nothing could possibly hurt her.

Maybe it couldn't. Maybe the haunting would be as invisible to her as it had been to my parents, who blamed everything on my "overactive" imagination.

Maybe. But I didn't think so.

As the door shut behind Katie the glass in the windows shivered. And so did I.

"Sally?" I said, calling to my little sister. "We better go in, too."

That's when I noticed that something was wrong with Sally's face. Her expression was stiff and her eyes were blank. As if she was in a trance or something.

A chill zapped me.

"Sally?" My voice was shaky.

Sally's head jerked to one side and then the other, like a puppet. Her eyes smoldered and glowed.

I fought the urge to leap away from her.

Then she opened her mouth and spoke. "I'm not Sally."

The voice that came out of her mouth was rough, as if it hadn't been used in a long time. And it had a hollow ring. As if it was coming from the inside of an empty tomb.

Sally's face scowled at me and the strange voice growled again. "My name is Bobby and I'm dead," she said.

I was paralyzed. I wanted to run. I wanted to scream.

My little sister was possessed!

2

Her face was like a mask. A mask that looked just like my little sister. Except for the eyes.

"Sally?" I said. "Please talk to me."

Her face scowled at me. Out of her mouth came that strange rough voice again. "I'm not Sally. My name is Bobby and I'm dead, dead, dead!"

She danced away, taunting me.

"Where's my sister?" I demanded.

I recognized the voice coming from Sally. I'd heard it night after night, crying in the hallway outside my room. It was the voice of a child ghost and I had never figured out what it wanted.

But lately I suspected what it wanted was Sally. And now it had her.

"My name is Bobby," it repeated, and Sally danced farther away from me.

I shivered, remembering when I'd first seen the ghost. It was the first day we arrived. We were driving up the long driveway under the tall whispery pines and I saw his pale, sad face.

A little boy peering at us from the attic windows. Little Bobby, who'd been dead for years and years.

Of course, no one believed me then.

They still didn't believe me. And the ghost had been careful to make sure they wouldn't. Now he had taken possession of my sister.

"Let me talk to Sally," I demanded, my voice cracking with fright.

Bobby wasn't an evil ghost, I told myself. At least Sally never thought so. She thought he was just a sad little boy who wanted to be her invisible friend. So what if he'd been dead for years?

So what if nobody else could see him? She could.

Maybe if I could keep him talking I could make him realize what a bad thing he was doing. "I want to talk to Sally, Bobby, where is she?"

Sally pressed her lips together tight. Or Bobby pressed her lips together. I was getting nowhere.

My head was spinning with a million different thoughts.

Bobby must have heard my parents talking about going away to Mayfield on a job and leaving me and Sally alone with a baby-sitter. A seventeen-year-old, red-haired girl who giggled at the idea of ghosts.

He must have been waiting for this chance.

Maybe he'd made friends with Sally just so she'd get to trust him. Then when the moment was right he seized her body and took it over.

Maybe he'd moved in permanently! The idea of this dead thing speaking from inside my sister made me feel like I'd swallowed a chunk of road-kill.

"Look, Bobby, tell me what you want," I said, inching closer. "I can help you if I know what you want."

"Hey, Jason! Sally!"

It was our baby-sitter Katie. She was supposed to be upstairs unpacking. Instead here she was leaning out the front door, grinning at us like she wanted to be friends. Her thick red hair fanned across her shoulders like a halo.

"Come on in and have a snack or something," Katie suggested.

"Uh, in a minute," I started to say. How could I tell her what had happened to my little sister?

Just then a ferocious scowl came over Sally's face. Blood rushed to her cheeks and her eyes seemed to glow with fire.

Something terrible was about to happen.

I reached out to grab Sally, but she was too fast for me.

She let out a scream of rage and charged straight at the baby-sitter.

3

The thing that ran up the steps after the baby-sitter wasn't my sister, it was a small demon.

"Look out!" I shouted.

But Katie just stood there. Her friendly smile went kind of limp, like she couldn't believe what was happening as Sally's hard little fists smacked her in the knees.

"Hey!" Katie cried out. "Hey, what are you doing?"

Sally was punching and kicking and scratching like a fierce little animal, and the poor baby-sitter didn't know what to do.

I had to save her — and Sally, too. I ran up the porch steps and grabbed my little sister from behind. Not so rough that I hurt her, but strong enough to pin her arms.

See, I didn't want to hurt her. After all, Sally was just a little kid. So I just tried to stop her from hitting the baby-sitter.

That's when she turned around and smacked me, hard, right in the stomach.

Ooof, the air went out of me and I sat down, holding my stomach. Sally ran off, disappearing inside the house.

"Hey, are you okay?" Katie knelt down, checking me out.

I nodded, struggling to get my breath back.

"What's wrong with your sister?" she asked.

"You don't want to know," I panted.

"Of course I do," she said. "I'm supposed to be in charge of you two until your parents get back."

Just then I heard Sally's little feet running across the kitchen floor. She was heading for the back door!

"Hurry!" I said. "We've got to stop her!"

I started running. Horrible thoughts exploded in my brain. What if Bobby did something terrible? What if he made my sister run into the lake, or out in front of a car?

Then she'd be like him forever. Another little ghost haunting this big creepy house.

I made myself run faster. "No, Sally! Stop!" I cried desperately.

I reached the kitchen just as Sally whipped the back door open.

She was too fast for me. In a second she'd be gone.

4

Sally bolted out the back door and disappeared around the side of the house.

My heart was in my throat as I pounded after her.

She was so fast! Faster than Sally should be. But somehow I had to catch her.

I whipped around the side of the house and saw her instantly. She had leaped up somehow and caught the lowest branch of the cherry tree. Her little legs wiggled as she struggled to pull herself up.

The cherry tree was Bobby's favorite place. He'd gotten Sally up into it once before.

I clenched my teeth against the memory and ran harder. Sally had been up so high, teetering on a skinny branch. And then she'd fallen.

Somehow I'd caught her. I still wasn't sure how, though I'd always thought Bobby helped. The way I figured it Bobby had wanted her to fall, to be his little friend forever. But at the last second, he saved her.

Now he was going to try again.

My lungs were bursting but I managed to shout. "Sally," I yelled. "Stop!"

Her head turned and her hand slipped from the branch. She tumbled to the ground and lay still.

"Sally!" My breath was rasping in my throat. I skidded to a stop and dropped down beside her.

"Ow," said Sally. She started to push herself up. "I'm bleeding," she said in a stricken voice.

Sally's voice! The eyes that looked back at me belonged to Sally, not the ghost. My little sister was back! Relief flooded me and I grabbed her and gave her a big hug.

"Are you okay?" I said, inspecting her knee, where she'd scraped it on the tree.

"What's going on? Is Sally all right?"

I turned around to see Katie approaching with a worried look, like she thought my four-year-old sister might leap up and attack her again.

"She skinned her knee," I said. "But she's back to being herself at least, right, Sally?"

I rose and picked Sally up to head back to the house.

Kate gave us a very weird look. She probably figured the whole family was crazy.

The truth was going to be even harder to believe.

Back in the kitchen I put Sally down in a chair at the table.

"We'd better wash off that knee and get you a Band-Aid," said Katie, obviously glad to have something to do.

Sally looked up at me. "Bobby was scared," she said. Then she looked at Katie who was hovering with a wet towel. "I guess Bobby doesn't like baby-sitters."

"Who's Bobby?" Katie asked brightly.

"He's my friend," said Sally.

Here we go, I thought.

I took a deep breath. "Bobby's a ghost," I said.

5

"A ghost," Katie repeated slowly. "And now he's possessed your little sister. Like *The Exorcist*, right?"

I remembered that movie. Something about a little girl who gets taken over by devils who make green vomit shoot out of her mouth while her head spins around in a circle.

"No, no," I said. "Bobby's not evil. He's a little boy who died here a long time ago. Sally's made friends with him but as soon as my parents left, he took over her body. See, it was really Bobby who attacked you like that."

Katie stared at me, water from the wet towel dripping down her arm.

"He's never done anything like that before," I said. "It scared me."

"I was sharing," Sally explained, frowning.

Katie made a face. "Is this a joke or what? I'm still waiting for the punch line, Jason."

"No joke. Really. Last night I thought we might

12

be killed. Or sucked into another dimension. It was horrible."

Katie rolled her eyes. "Yeah, right. And today your parents go off on some emergency job on the other side of the state — "

"A firehouse," I said.

"What?" said Katie.

"My parents designed a firehouse in Mayfield. They're architects. That's why we're here. They're designing a town complex for Hartsville. But they got this call from Mayfield that some changes need to be made in the firehouse design — " I stopped.

This wasn't going right at all.

I tried again. "My mom and dad can't see the ghost, or hear him, either. Sally sees him and I can see him sometimes. At night I hear him crying. And there's this skeleton thing in a black cloak with glowing eyes. I think it may be the ghost of an old witch who died here. They never found the body."

Katie sighed. "Your parents were right," she said. You *do* have an active imagination. Too bad I don't believe in ghosts."

"You should go," said Sally, making a pruny face. "Bobby doesn't like baby-sitters."

"That does it." Katie finally noticed the towel dripping down her wrist. She threw it in the sink. "I've seen kids get up to a lot of tricks but you two are something else. Dreaming up this elaborate story just to scare me. Well, it won't work!"

As she flounced out of the kitchen I knew we were on our own. And it didn't make me feel strong or grown-up or anything like that. Not at all. It made me feel alone.

Sally got down from her chair, ready to start playing again. She didn't seem to be worried about anything — maybe she didn't even realize she'd been possessed!

"Sally, wait."

She looked at me, her eyes full of trust.

I put my hand on her shoulder and looked into her face. "Did you let Bobby take you over before? Did you give him permission or did he just do it?"

Sally shrugged off my hand. "I want Winky," she said. Winky was her stuffed bunny.

"Sally, wait a minute. Do you think Bobby will do that to you again?"

"Bobby is my friend," Sally said, acting stubborn and not wanting to look at me. She started for the door.

"I know he's your friend," I said desperately. "But Sally, could you keep him out if you wanted to?"

Sally hunched her shoulders up around her neck and didn't answer.

The door swung closed behind her, leaving me alone.

A faint chill tickled the back of my neck. As if something was watching me from the shadows.

I turned but there was nothing there.

Then it happened.

Softly at first, then louder, weird, cackling old-lady laughter rose up inside the walls.

Very faint, but I could hear it. Ghost laughter. And the joke was on me.

6

I decided not to let Sally out of my sight the rest of the day. She wanted to play outside under the cherry tree, so I hung around, watching her do make-believe stuff with Winky and her other dolls and stuffed animals.

It was boring but to tell you the truth, I was glad to be out of the house. Glad to be away from the noises in the walls and the cackling laughter that only happened when I was alone.

After a while Katie came outside to check up on us.

"What a lovely cherry tree," she said, shading her eyes against the sun. "It looks really old."

A gust of wind came up and scattered the last of the tree's blossoms.

"I don't think I've ever seen a cherry tree with blooms so late. It's nearly the end of June," said Katie.

I didn't tell her what I suspected — that the ghost had played in that weird old cherry tree when he was still alive. And that he still haunted it now that he was a ghost.

"Hey, think quick!"

I ducked as a baseball went whipping by my head, just missing me. It was Steve, my friend from next door. "Come on," he said. "Let's go down to the ball field and practice."

Steve was an awesome pitcher and I was okay on third base — a pretty good hitter, if I do say so myself. I wanted to play ball so badly I could taste it. It would be great to get away for a while and leave this spooky place behind. But I couldn't.

"I've got to keep an eye on my sister," I told Steve.

"Go ahead," Katie encouraged me. "I'll watch Sally."

"I don't really feel like it," I said, scuffing my sneakered toe in the grass.

"Come on," said Katie tauntingly. "You're not scared Sally will be possessed again while you're gone, are you?"

"Possessed?" echoed Steve, wide-eyed. He was a little bigger than I, built solid. Ghost talk made him look round all over — round eyes and round mouth in a round face.

Katie laughed. "Jason's got quite an imagination. He tried to scare me this morning pretending Sally was possessed by a ghost."

"Wow!" said Steve, looking at me. "The little boy ghost or the old lady ghost?"

17

Katie's eyes blazed. "Not you, too!" She tossed her head, swinging her shoulder-length, red hair, and stalked off into the house.

Steve raised his eyebrows at me. "I guess she doesn't believe in spooks, huh?"

"Not yet," I said, glancing back up at the house.

Steve and I played catch for a while, right there in the yard. He kept rearing back and throwing hard and it was all I could do to get the glove in front of the ball.

"Definitely big league material," Steve said, very pleased with himself. "Don't worry, you can still be my friend when I get voted best pitcher in the bigs."

"Thanks a bunch," I said. "You'll probably charge for autographs."

While we practiced, Sally kept busy by herself, holding up Winky and talking to that dumb stuffed rabbit.

"Winky," I heard her say. "Tell Bobby to come out and play."

Great! I was trying to get rid of the ghost and she wanted to play with him!

Just then Steve's mother called him.

"Gotta go," he said, picking up the ball. "See you later, alligator."

"In a while, crocodile."

Steve was barely out of sight when Sally announced that she was going inside. "Bobby's lonesome," she explained, picking up her dolls.

I was left alone, standing under the cherry tree, looking up at the house. The old building seemed to loom over me, and the windows were like eyes.

Blank eyes, hiding terrible secrets.

I shuddered. What was wrong with me — it was still broad daylight, and bad things never happened until after dark, right?

That's what I told myself. But as I stared up at those blank windows, suddenly something moved. At first it was blurry, and then it came into sharp focus.

A small, pale-looking boy was up there in the attic, looking down at me. He was dressed in old-fashioned clothes, and as I stared up at him he raised his little hand and waved at me.

Bobby. The dead boy.

7

"Spaghetti anyone?" said Katie, holding up a ladle like a tennis racket.

"Don't mind if I do," I said, rubbing my hands together.

A couple of hours had passed and it was time for supper. I hadn't mentioned seeing the ghost in the attic window. Katie would just think I was making it up, and there was no way to prove it to her.

Besides, I didn't even want to think about the dumb old ghost. All this spooky stuff was making my life miserable. Haunted houses sound cool in made-up stories, but if you have to live in one it's no fun at all.

Not when that bony hand reaches out from under the bed and grabs you in the night.

"This will be fun," said Katie, getting down a big pot for the spaghetti.

You could tell that Katie was trying hard. This was the first time she'd ever been an overnight baby-sitter and she was taking the job seriously. The last thing she wanted was for my parents to find out she couldn't handle it, so she wanted to make friends with me and Sally.

"We're in this together," she said brightly. "We might as well have fun."

She filled the pot with water and was lugging it to the stove when she tripped.

"Look out!"

The pot tipped over, dousing her with cold water. "Ugh," she said, looking down at her soaked Levi's. "Well, that was my own fault. I'll have to go up to my room and change."

I managed to refill the pot and get it on the stove while she was gone. Mr. Helpful, that's me. I'd just turned the burner on when I heard running feet coming from upstairs.

"Jayyyy-sonnnnnnnn!" someone screamed.

It was Katie. She came skidding into the kitchen, her eyes blazing with anger.

"You little wretch!" she said. "How *could* you!?"

Then she burst into tears.

I was so startled I could only stare at her.

"Don't play innocent with me, Jason," she said, wiping away her tears. "I want an explanation."

"What are you talking about?" I said. "I don't understand. Really."

Something in my face must have convinced her at least a little bit. Her shoulders relaxed and she spun around and headed back upstairs. "Come with me," she ordered.

With Sally tagging behind, I followed Katie upstairs, down the hall to the room Mom had given her. It was a nice room with rose-patterned wallpaper and a big four-poster bed. A girl's room.

I stopped short in the open doorway. It *had* been a nice room — but now it looked like a bomb had gone off.

Her clothes were strewn all over the room, balled up on every inch of floor. Blouses and T-shirts were flung over the rocking chair and a fancy-looking sweater was mooshed up, hanging from the corner of a painting on the wall.

I shook my head. "It wasn't me. I haven't been up here for hours."

"Oh? Who was it then?" she challenged. "I suppose you're going to tell me it was the ghost."

I nodded. "I didn't believe it, either, at first. I don't blame you for thinking it was me even though I would never do anything like this. But it must have been Bobby."

"A ghost? Don't be ridiculous."

"I think Bobby's trying to get you out of the house," I said. "If we could only figure out why . . ."

I let my voice trail off. Katie didn't believe a word I was saying. I couldn't blame her, really. Before we came to this house, I never believed in ghosts, either — so why should she believe me?

"I don't know what you kids have against me," she said. "But I'm going to stick it out, whatever you do. So you might as well get used to me. I'm not so bad. Really."

Sally just stared up at her with wondering eyes.

I mumbled a protest. "We're not trying to get rid of you."

Katie turned away with a shaky smile. "Forget it. Now let's go have dinner."

We trooped back downstairs.

The water was boiling. Steam rattled the lid and escaped in big jets out the sides. "I'll put the spaghetti on," I said, trying to sound like it was no big deal.

But the truth was, you never knew what might happen in this house. Sometimes it played tricks, moving things around, and I didn't want the pot to tip over on Katie again, not when the water was boiling.

I opened the box of spaghetti, grabbed a fistful, and went to the stove.

Holding my body well back from the stove, I lifted the lid. The water was bubbling furiously and steam billowed up to the ceiling.

I dropped the spaghetti in and jumped back. I didn't realize I'd been holding my breath till I let it out.

"Let me give that a stir," said Katie.

Before I could stop her or even cry out a warning she lifted the lid and stuck in a long-handled spoon.

"There." She set the spoon on the counter and I let myself relax. Nothing had happened. The boiling water wasn't going to burn her.

Then Katie picked up the jar of spaghetti sauce. And as she started to tip it into a pan, the jar jerked out of her grasp.

Katie screamed. The jar landed with a crash on the floor. Glass and gloppy sauce spattered everywhere.

"It felt like it was yanked out of my hands!" cried Katie, staring at the mess.

Sally giggled.

I hushed her and grabbed fistfuls of paper towels. "It looked that way to me, too," I said, starting to shovel the mess into a dust pan. "Like something grabbed it."

Katie gave me a black look. "That's crazy. I dropped it, that's all. Must be nerves. It comes from being around you two and wondering what you'll get up to next."

I didn't say anything, just finished cleaning up the mess.

"Luckily there's another jar of sauce," said Katie, reaching for it.

I hunched my shoulders, expecting it to go flying against the wall. It didn't.

Katie twisted the lid but it wouldn't budge. She tried again, grunting with effort.

"Here," I said, glad to have an excuse to offer. "Let me." It was our last jar and I was hungry.

Katie shrugged. "I'll set the table."

I got the lid off and the sauce safely into a pan and on the stove while Katie took down a stack of dishes. She picked up the top plate to set it on the table.

It flew out of her hand, skimmed across the kitchen like a Frisbee, and smashed into the wall.

Frowning at the shattered pieces on the floor, Katie grasped the second plate. It shot away from her and smashed into the opposite wall.

Sally watched it all happen, smiling her secret smile.

"I don't understand this," Katie said, staring at the broken crockery. "I've never been such a klutz."

"Why don't you sit down with Sally," I suggested. "I'll get the food. It's just about ready anyway."

Moving like a sleepwalker, Katie got the broom and began sweeping up the broken plates. "It was weird," she said in a quiet, puzzled voice. "It was like they came alive in my hand."

Holding everything very tightly and moving very carefully, I got the plates and our dinner to the table. Nothing wiggled in my hand or tried to get away.

My stomach was growling fiercely. I heaped spaghetti on my plate and dumped on some sauce.

Just as I was putting the bowl of sauce down, the lights went out.

The kitchen was plunged into pitch blackness.

"What's that?" Katie whispered in the dark.

I heard a plate slither across the table. Then another.

It was starting. The house was coming alive.

8

A glass crashed to the floor.

It was pitch black — I couldn't see a thing. Plates clattered. Then there was another noise, a squishy splat kind of noise and someone screamed.

"STOP IT. Stop it, *please*."

Katie.

I started up out of my seat. I don't know what I was going to do — something, anything except just sit there — but just then the light came back on.

The first thing I saw was Katie, covered from head to foot in red gore. Gobs dripped down from her hair onto her cheeks. Her yellow blouse had turned the color of blood. She was breathing in little gasps and her blazing eyes were fixed on me.

"You!" she sputtered, sending red drops flying. "You!"

Just then I noticed the bowl in her lap. The sauce bowl. That was the source of all the gory, bloody-looking stuff. It had been emptied over her head, then dumped in her lap.

"You did this, Jason!" she said, pointing a finger at me.

"It wasn't me," I insisted. "I swear I didn't do it."

"Yeah, sure," Katie said disgustedly. "It was a ghost, right?"

"Bobby's a bad boy," said Sally sadly.

Katie gritted her teeth and glared. "Jason's the only bad boy around here," she said.

It was no use trying to talk sense to her. First, it was easier to blame me, and second, she looked so funny covered in spaghetti sauce, I was afraid I might burst out laughing.

We finally managed to eat our supper without anything else happening.

Katie calmed down a bit, but she still didn't trust me. When I offered to clean up the mess she said, "No way. You'll break every dish in the house and blame it on ghosts."

I got a couple of ice pops out of the freezer and took Sally out on the porch. Maybe with my sister outside, the house would leave us alone for a while.

We were on the porch for only a couple of minutes when a voice boomed out of the dark. "Jayy-sssonnnnnn!"

I recognized the voice right away. Steve, trying to sound spooky.

"Knock it off," I said. "The last thing we need around here is a practical joker."

Steve came up on the porch, grinning that big grin of his. He slapped me five and said, "This house must be getting to you, bud."

"You don't know the half of it," I said.

Just then the porch stair creaked. It was Lucy, who lived a couple of houses over. Lucy was twelve, like me and Steve, but while Steve was husky and solid, Lucy was tall and long-legged. She wore her dark ponytail pulled through the back of her baseball cap.

"Is it Bobby again?" she asked.

Lucy knew about the things that had been happening in the house and took the haunting seriously. She and Steve sat on the porch steps while I told them what had happened when Katie tried to make dinner.

"That sounds creepy," said Lucy, frowning thoughtfully at the top of her sandal. "What would Bobby have against her? What's she like?"

I shrugged. "She's okay. In fact, she's pretty nice. Except she's blaming everything on me."

"Maybe the ghost has something against teenage girls," Lucy suggested. "Or baby-sitters."

"Smart ghost," put in Steve, blowing a fart noise into his fist.

I was still laughing when a strange expression came over Lucy's face. "Hi," she said loudly, jumping up.

I turned and there was Katie in the doorway, freshly showered and changed. Her thick red hair was combed and even her freckles looked fresh-scrubbed.

But the look on her face was anything but sweet. She knew we'd been talking about her. She squinted her eyes at me and I felt a chill.

Suddenly I knew that crossing Katie could be dangerous.

9

Katie went out of her way to be nice to Steve and Lucy. She brought them ice pops and insisted they tell her all about themselves. Lucy's not much of a talker, but Steve made up for it by going on and on about what a good ballplayer he was, and how he was going to play pro ball when he grew up.

"The only thing I'm not sure about," Steve said, "is whether to sign with the American League or the National League."

"Depends on how well you bat," said Katie.

"What?"

"American League has the designated hitter, but in the National League the pitcher gets to hit, right?"

Steve whistled and looked impressed. A baby-sitter who knew about the DH rule!

"What about you, Lucy?" Katie asked. "What do you want to be?"

Lucy smiled shyly. "Maybe a scientist," she

said. "I'd like to investigate unexplained phenomena."

Katie just stared at her for a moment, then burst out laughing. "You mean like poltergeists and ghosts, I suppose?" She glanced over at me and shook her head. "You've all been bitten by this ghost bug, I guess. Well, before you start trying to scare me again, I'm going to have to call it a night. It's time for Sally to go to bed."

After Steve and Lucy said good night and left, we went back inside the house. The lights stayed on, there were no creaky noises, and the kitchen was spick-and-span again, as if nothing had happened.

"Thanks for being nice to my friends," I said.

Katie gave me a strange look and then laughed. "Why shouldn't I be nice? I'm a nice person, even if certain kids try to take advantage."

I sighed. She was just never going to believe I wasn't causing all the trouble!

Sally had been quiet all evening — her eyes were already half closed and I knew she was ready for bed. I took one hand and Katie took the other and we walked her upstairs to her bedroom. Katie helped her into her pajamas and for a little while she seemed happy and friendly, as if she was glad to have Katie around.

"When are Mommy and Daddy coming home?" Sally asked as she got into bed.

"In a few days," Katie promised. "Until then, we're going to have lots and lots of fun, okay?"

"Okay," Sally said.

Then the smile froze on her face and her eyes grew round. "Where's Winky?" she wailed. "I want my rabbit!"

Her stuffed toy with the floppy ears. She'd left it down on the porch.

"I'll get it," I volunteered.

As I ran down the stairs I noticed something strange. The lights were out downstairs. And I distinctly remembered that they'd been left on.

It was so dark. And the tall grandfather clock jumped out at me from the shadowy hallway. Not really, but that's how it looked.

It was only a broken clock but it gave me the creeps. As if it was watching me from behind the clock face.

Go for it, I urged myself.

I ran past the clock and out the door to the porch.

The porch light was out, too. The wind was sighing through the grass, and the lawn looked pale and silvery in the moonlight.

Something moved.

Creak creak creak.

The porch rocker was moving. Creaking back and forth. The rocker where Sally had been sitting.

More than anything, I wanted to run back inside and lock the door. Let Sally cry herself to sleep — was that such a big deal?

But I couldn't do that. I had to get Winky or my little sister would keep us awake all night.

The chair stopped rocking. The way the shadows fell across the porch, I couldn't tell if Winky was in the chair where Sally had left it. But something was there, that was for sure.

I took a deep breath, gritted my teeth, and ran up to the chair.

The shadows shifted and there it was.

Winky. It was just a stuffed toy, but it looked almost like it was alive.

I grabbed it, half expecting it to sink fangs into my hand, but nothing happened. It flopped around in my hand, totally harmless.

Letting out my breath, I ran back into the house and flipped on the hall lights.

I tucked it under my arm and ran up the stairs two at a time.

Sally was sitting up in bed, holding out her arms. "Winky!" she cried.

"Not a minute too soon," said Katie with a sigh.

Sally's anxious look disappeared when I gave her the bunny. She snuggled back under the covers and I tucked Winky in beside her. "My bunny," she said contentedly.

As I started to leave, Katie leaned over the bed.

"Can I give you a good-night kiss?" she asked, smoothing the hair off Sally's forehead.

I looked back. Just in time to see Sally's face change.

Suddenly her cheeks bunched and went bright red.

Her eyes seemed to shoot sparks. Her forehead bulged.

"No!" she spat, in the same strange, rough voice that had come out of her when Mom and Dad drove away. "I hate you!" she screamed at Katie. "I hate you!"

Katie backed away, totally at a loss.

"Go away," the ghostly voice shouted through Sally's wide-straining mouth. "Get out of my house!"

10

My little sister was snarling like an animal.

I tapped Katie on the arm and said, "You better leave!"

Katie looked scared, but she wasn't ready to give up. "No way!" she said, turning to me with a scowl. "I'm not leaving, no matter how hard you try!"

All I wanted to do was protect her from the ghost, but she thought I was trying to chase her out of the house.

"Please," I begged her, "wait out in the hall, or downstairs. Let me try and get Sally calmed down."

Katie wasn't convinced, but Sally was getting more and more frantic, so she finally left the room.

As soon as she was out of sight, Sally's body seemed to deflate. I dropped to my knees beside the bed and gripped her shoulders. "Sally!" I demanded. "Sally, I know you're in there! Talk to me!"

The blaze died out of Sally's eyes and they returned to their normal little-girl blue.

"Sally?" I said softly.

She rubbed her eyes with the back of a small fist. "I didn't know Bobby was going to do that," she said in a small, troubled voice. "Bobby's a bad boy, isn't he?"

I hugged her to me, feeling my heart thumping. What were we going to do?

"It's all right now, Sally," I said. "He's gone."

"Bobby doesn't like baby-sitters," said Sally, yawning.

When I set her head back on the pillow, she was already asleep.

Outside in the hallway, Katie waited, looking worried.

"It's all right," I said. "Sally's herself again."

"She was like a totally different person," Katie said shakily.

"That's Bobby," I explained. Maybe Katie would believe me now. I could certainly use her help.

But Katie put her hands on her hips and frowned at me. "I don't know what you think you're up to," she said, "but getting your little sister to play along with your jokes is really sick."

My heart sank — she still thought it was my fault. "It wasn't me," I said. "You've got to believe me. It's the ghost, or the house, or something I haven't figured out yet — but it's not me."

"I hope you're proud of yourself," said Katie as she stalked off toward the stairs, shaking her head. "What you're doing to that poor little girl is a crime and don't think I won't be telling your parents!"

What could I say? I knew how lame it sounded, blaming everything on a ghost. But it just happened to be true, even if none of the grown-ups could see or hear what was going on.

So I didn't say anything. I just stood there watching Katie walk away. And that's when it happened.

Evil laughter echoed deep inside the walls. That mean, cackling witch laugh I'd heard before. The laughter Katie couldn't hear.

But this time she stopped in her tracks and turned back to look at me. "Cut it out," she said. "You think that stupid laughter is going to scare me? What is it, a tape recording of a Halloween laugh?" Katie rolled her eyes and tossed her head, turning her back. "Spare me."

Things were bad. It was night and things might get much, much worse.

Yes, things were bad all right, but for some reason I felt like jumping for joy.

Because unlike my parents, Katie could hear the haunted laughter coming from the walls!

I wasn't alone after all!

11

I was sound asleep, dreaming about a baseball game, when a bolt of lightning woke me up.

The flash of light made my bedroom look inside out, like a photographic negative. Then it was pitch black again and I was sitting straight up in my bed with my heart pounding hard enough to bust my ribs.

I couldn't see a thing.

But I could hear things.

Outside the leaves were rustling. A branch banged against the house.

And then KER-WHAM! thunder exploded like a bomb, shaking the whole house.

As lightning flashed I saw a face looking at me.

A pale, tense, terrified face. The mouth was open, like it wanted to scream but couldn't make a sound.

The face was me.

My own frightened face reflected in the mirror on the closet door.

Suddenly the sky broke open and it was raining. Raining so hard it sounded like all the oceans of the world were crashing over the roof. The rain poured over the window glass as the lightning flashed again.

It was only a storm. A summer storm. I was safe inside. Nothing could hurt me.

My pounding heart started to slow. I lay my head back down on the pillow and closed my eyes, determined to go back to sleep.

Then I heard footsteps in the hallway.

Little running footsteps. I pulled the covers over my head. I was not going to get up, no matter what.

Another jolt of lightning glowed right through the blanket, making my bedroom walls look as white as bone.

Something knocked on the door.

I peeked out from under the covers.

Was the doorknob wiggling or was that my imagination?

The knocking noise came again, louder.

This was how it always started. Noises in the hall. Scratching fingers outside my door.

It wanted me to open the door and let it in. Then the horror would start all over.

Slowly the door opened wider and wider. I scrambled to get out of bed. The thing wasn't going to find me defenseless.

My legs were caught in the bed clothes. I

couldn't get free. I kicked and pushed frantically but it seemed to take forever.

At last my legs were untangled. I looked toward the door. It was wide open now.

A dark shape came through the doorway and glided into the room.

Coming to get me.

Quickly I dropped to my knees beside the bed. There was a baseball bat under the bed if only I could find it in the dark. My fingers groped blindly.

No bat.

The thing in the doorway was a black shadow against the light from the hall. It was small but seemed to be growing larger.

At last my fingers closed around the handle of the bat.

I stood up.

The shadowy figure lurched toward me. Reaching out, trying to grab me.

Trembling, I raised the bat.

41

12

"**J**ason, help!"

My arm turned to rubber and my knees to water.

I collapsed onto my bed. I'd nearly brained my little sister with a baseball bat!

This house was getting to me. As if it *wanted* me to hurt my sister.

Sally tugged at my arm. "Come on, Jason. Hurry!"

"Sally, what's wrong?" I asked. "What are you doing out of bed? You're not afraid of the thunder, are you?"

"No, no, no," said Sally, stamping her feet. "Bobby says you have to come. Right now, before it's too late. Come on!"

"No way," I said firmly, pulling my arm free. "I'm not going anywhere."

"But you have to!" Sally urged. "You have to come downstairs. It's important."

Had Sally forgotten what happens at night in

this house? Well, I wouldn't remind her — she was already scared enough. But you'd have to be brain-dead to wander around this place after midnight.

"Jason, you have to, you have to." Sally was near tears.

"But why?" I took hold of her arms. "What is it that can't wait until morning?"

"Bobby needs you," said Sally. "Bobby can't do it by himself."

"What about Katie?" I suggested. "She's the baby-sitter. She's responsible, right?"

Sally looked down at the floor. "Bobby hates the baby-sitter."

I gave in. I always give in. When Sally wants something, she never gives up. Just yammers on forever until you agree. A definite one-track mind.

"I'll go as far as the top of the stairs," I said. "That's it. Then it's back to bed for both of us."

Sally considered this. "All right," she said, taking my hand.

The storm hadn't let up a bit.

The hall light flickered and went out.

But Sally forged ahead, pulling me along.

The top of the stairs was as black as a witch's cat. I couldn't see a thing — and I wasn't going any farther.

"Everything seems fine to me," I said, trying to sound like I meant it.

It was true enough, at the moment. At least

there were no weird ghostly lights and no furniture flying through the air like before.

Something sounded funny, though.

I couldn't quite pinpoint the problem. But there was a vague unease tickling at me.

Something inside the house was . . . wrong. But I shrugged it off.

"Okay," I said, squeezing Sally's hand. "Back to bed."

At that instant a bolt of lightning crashed so close it lit up the whole downstairs.

I stared in shock.

"No," I cried. "No!"

And then I dropped Sally's hand and was flying down the stairs.

13

As I reached the bottom of the stairs, a gust of wind blasted me backwards. I staggered, soaked to the skin immediately.

I reached for a lamp and turned the switch. Nothing.

Another flash of lightning.

I couldn't believe my eyes. Every window stood wide open.

The storm was pouring inside. Rain lashed at the antiques Mom was always warning me about.

I could imagine her face when she saw what the water had done to all this fancy furniture that didn't belong to us.

But I couldn't imagine telling her a ghost did this just to get me in trouble.

Still, I hesitated. I was shy of the windows in this house. I kept remembering how the window in my bedroom nearly came down on my neck like a guillotine. Maybe it was silly but I always thought the window was disappointed it had missed.

The house was trying to trick me again.

I was scared but the idea made me mad. This creepy old place kept trying to get me in trouble, and now it was fixing things so I'd get blamed for ruining all the furniture!

Over my dead body.

With the hard rain stinging my face, I ran to the nearest window and grabbed hold, pulling down with all my might.

It wouldn't budge. The rain pelted me in buckets as I tugged, banged, and strained.

Something warned me.

Maybe a slight vibration in the window frame. I jumped backwards.

The window crashed down, shaking the wall and knocking a lamp to the floor.

I shuddered — a close call.

Then I ran to the next window. The wet curtain flapped around my face. Yuck! I shied away and it slithered around my neck.

I tried to jerk my head free but the silky wet cloth clung tighter, squeezing my throat.

I clawed at it frantically.

The ends whipped at my face in the wind.

I was choking!

I worked two fingers under the cloth and pried it away from my throat.

The wind slacked off briefly. Working fast, I

loosened its grip and slipped my head out from under.

I slumped against the wall, the breath wheezing through my bruised throat.

That window could just stay open for the time being.

But no, I thought. I wouldn't give up that easily. Spooked by a curtain, how silly could you get!

More determined than ever, I gripped the top of the window frame and pulled with all my might. It stayed stuck, rain splattering me in the face, blinding me.

I hung with my full weight and banged on the frame. It wouldn't budge.

Finally, defeated, I gave up.

And the window shot down so suddenly I fell back onto the mouse-colored rug my mother liked so much. It squelched under me. That valuable, ugly old thing was wet as a sponge.

Lightning flashed again.

I ground my teeth and ran to the next window.

But this time just as I touched the window frame there was a hideous scream.

A piercing shriek of fury.

It came from the top of the stairs. Where I'd left Sally.

As I whipped around in the darkness there was a long, mad screech. Something big flew down the stairs, screaming my name.

It was headed right for me.

14

I heard it stumble at the bottom of the stairs.
There was a harsh growl of pain.

I pressed myself against the open window, trying to see. Rain dribbled down my neck.

It got up. And stumbled again, like it couldn't see in the dark.

That was strange. Why would a ghost mind the dark?

I heard it scuttling around on the floor like a bug with a broken back.

Then it spoke, much closer than I expected.

"Jason! How could you!"

"Katie?" I was so relieved I started to laugh. "Is that you?"

"Oh, you think this is funny, do you? You're sick, you know that?"

There was another flash like a camera strobe and I could see how it looked to Katie in the cold blue light, with all the windows open, the rain blowing in. And me, who might be opening a window instead of closing it.

She darted toward a window.

"No!" I shouted.

Not that she'd listen to me.

Lightning jolted again and I saw Katie grasping the top of the window, pulling with all her strength, her head bowed under the open frame, her neck —

Springing toward her in the dark, I yelled at her to get back, knowing she was too stubborn and mad to listen to me.

It took forever to cross the room — I kept bumping into things, as if the house didn't want me to get to Katie.

In the dimness between flashes of lightning I saw the top of the window give a little shiver.

I was too far away to save her.

I threw myself through the air.

Slamming into Katie sideways, I shoved her out of the way just as the window crashed down.

It slammed shut so hard, the whole house shook.

I pushed myself up off the floor and took a deep breath. Katie didn't move.

"Wow," she said softly, her voice small. "That was close."

"I tried to tell you," I said. "This is a dangerous place."

A sudden gust of wind blew rain over us both. But if I thought Katie was going to be grateful that I'd saved her life, I was wrong.

"How could you!" she said through clenched teeth. "This will get me in trouble for sure. Your mother told me about all the antiques in this place. They'll be ruined!"

She groped her way toward the last window in the room. I ran to get in front of her.

"Let me do it," I pleaded. "They're all stuck. But I can tell when they're about to let go. Stand back!"

I flung myself at the window and pulled. As it came crashing down I stumbled and fell backwards over a chair.

The air was suddenly still inside the house, although it continued to rattle the window glass from outside.

"Are there any candles?" Katie asked.

"I have a flashlight," I said, getting up from the floor. "But it's upstairs on my dresser."

"We better get it and clean up this mess."

Sally was waiting for us at the bottom of the stairs. I could just make her out. She was holding something in her lap. I ruffled her hair. "You okay, kid?"

Sally nodded. "Winky doesn't like the thunder," she said, holding up her bunny.

I waited, keeping Sally company while Katie went up to get the flashlight.

The beam of it blinded me as Katie came back down the stairs. She shone the light around the living room. "What a mess," she said. "We'll be up all night trying to clean this up." She shot me a baffled look. "I don't understand what you were trying to do, opening all those windows in the middle of a rainstorm."

"I know you won't believe me, Katie, but this house really is haunted. I didn't open the windows. It was the ghost, Bobby."

"No," cried Sally loudly. "It wasn't Bobby. He wanted you to fix it. That's why I came into your room!"

My heart sank. If not Bobby, then it was the other ghost — the old witch with the skeleton hands and the glowing eyes.

But if Bobby's ghost wanted me to stop the old witch, then they weren't doing their haunting together.

And if they weren't together then what I had feared last night was probably true. Bobby and the old witch were fighting some great battle — and we were caught right in the middle.

15

The next day Katie convinced me to go play baseball with my friends.

"Maybe the windows really weren't your fault," she said. "Maybe you were sleepwalking. Or something."

We'd been up half the night sopping up water and using Katie's hair dryer on the chair cushions and rugs. I really needed a break.

"Go ahead," Katie said. "I'll look out for Sally."

Maybe it was safe for me to leave, now that it was daytime. The really bad stuff happened at night, right?

"Go on," Katie said, giving me a weary smile. "Hit a home run. Hit *two* home runs."

"Thanks," I said. "Maybe I will."

So I took off for the ball field with Steve and Lucy, and once the house was out of sight, it was like a great weight lifted from my shoulders.

All I could think about was how great it was to swing the bat and hit that little white ball.

Steve was pitching, of course. But this time I got the better of him.

"Batter, batter, no batter," he chanted, going into his windup.

The ball came flying out over the plate, going about a hundred miles an hour.

I gritted my teeth and swung as hard as I could.

And I hit that ball so sweet and clean I could hardly feel it. It felt like the bat was glowing in my hands. And the ball was flying back so fast that Steve had to duck out of the way.

The ball kept going. Rising and rising, heading deep into the outfield.

Lucy tried to run it down. She ran to the deepest part of center field and jumped just as it went over her head.

She reached up, trying for the ball, but it was too high.

Home run to deep center! I'd never hit the ball so far in my life!

I razzed Steve as I did a slow trot around the bases. He just shook his head and threw his glove on the ground.

"Fastball down the middle," he moaned. "That's my best pitch."

Lucy came running in from the outfield and slapped me ten. "Aw right! Way to go! Nice hit!"

"He must have got lucky," Steve complained. "Nobody can hit my fastball."

"Get used to it," Lucy said with a grin.

Steve moaned and groaned all the way back from the ball field, but by the time we got to his house he was grinning and shaking his head. "I guess I better learn to throw a spitter," he said.

Lucy and Steve both went home for lunch, which left me alone for the first time that day.

That's when it hit me. I'd been selfish, going off to play ball with my buds. While I was out having a good time, my little sister was left alone with a baby-sitter who didn't have a clue.

I started walking faster, heading for the house on Cherry Street.

The minute I stepped into the shadow of the tall whispery pines, an icy chill ran down my spine. I was suddenly cold. Very cold.

As if the house was breathing in my warmth as it pulled me closer. As if the house was feeding off me, drinking in the energy I brought it from outside.

The house was growing stronger while I grew weaker.

"Don't be a meathead," I said out loud, kicking at the pine needles under my feet. "You're not even in the house yet, how could it hurt you?"

Hurrying along, I tried thinking about how cool it had been to hit that home run off a great pitcher like Steve, but the house seemed to snatch at my thoughts and unravel them.

The old house was watching me and practically splitting its sides laughing. I could almost hear it taunting me, saying *"Jay-sonnnnnnn. I know something you don't know."*

My feet, shuffling the dry pine needles, began moving faster.

The house had been waiting for me to leave. It had *wanted* me to go play ball.

"This is really, really stupid," I muttered to myself.

But my feet picked up the pace anyway. By the time I reached the back porch, I was running full blast.

I stopped a second to catch my breath. Wouldn't want Katie to think I didn't trust her to watch Sally for a couple hours.

I opened the kitchen door and went inside, expecting to find Katie and Sally just sitting down to lunch.

Nobody there.

The breakfast dishes were still on the table.

"Sally! Katie!" I called out.

No answer. Maybe they'd gone for a walk. Down to the lake, maybe.

Sure. That was it. And I'd have to fix my own lunch. No big deal.

As I opened the refrigerator door and looked inside, there was a loud thud behind me.

I whipped around. Nothing there.

Then I heard a croaking noise. Like somebody couldn't breathe. Like they were gasping for breath.

It was coming from behind the basement door.

My heart was hammering.

"*Jason!*" called a strange, cracked voice from behind the basement door. "*Help me! Please help me! Open the door!*"

Forget it. The house was trying to trick me again. I never, ever wanted to go anywhere near that dark and haunted basement.

"No way," I said to myself. "Don't be a sucker."

But my feet weren't listening. They were taking me closer and closer to the basement door.

"*Help,*" begged a faint voice. "*Let me out!*"

BAM! A fist rattled the door.

"*Jay-sssson, please let me out.*"

There was something about the voice. Something familiar.

"*Jaysssonnnnnn!*"

I unlocked the door and yanked it open.

Katie fell out in a heap at my feet. "Thank God," she croaked. "Water!"

I quickly got her a glass of water. She gulped it down and then sighed deeply.

"I heard a noise," she said, getting her voice back. "A weird noise in the basement. I just went down for a second to check on it. Then the door slammed behind me. It locked from the outside, so I was trapped."

She narrowed her eyes at me. "*Someone* must have thought it was a pretty funny joke. I've been calling and yelling for hours."

"Hours?" The hair on the back of my neck prickled. "You've been down there for hours?"

She gulped some more water and looked around. "Where's your sister? Isn't she with you?"

I shook my head. "No. She didn't answer when I called," I said slowly.

"Come on, Jason, the joke's over," said Katie.

"But I couldn't have locked you in the basement. I've been playing ball with my friends — you can check on that," I said.

Slowly it dawned on Katie that I was telling the truth. "Then if Sally's not with you, where is she?" she asked.

We ran upstairs.

As if, after all this time, speed would make any difference.

My sister's bedroom door was closed.

"Sally!" I called.

Katie turned the knob. The door was locked.

Sally would never lock her door. She wasn't allowed, for one thing. And that old lock didn't even have a key.

Katie banged on the door.

"Sally! Are you in there?"

Sally didn't answer.

16

What were we going to do? My sister was locked in her room in a house where anything could happen — and frequently did.

"Have you got a screwdriver?" asked Katie, examining the lock.

"A screwdriver?"

"Preferably a long, skinny one."

I dashed back downstairs to my parents' office where my dad keeps his tools. The room with its empty drafting tables and long-necked lamps looked dusty, as if no one had been there for months.

Hard to believe it was only yesterday they'd left.

On my way back upstairs I heard Katie still calling Sally through the door.

No response.

My stomach felt hollow. It had been hours since anyone had seen Sally.

Katie looked worried. "If your sister's in there, she's not answering," she said, and took the screwdriver from my hand. "But why would she lock me in the cellar?"

Katie forced the door open with the screwdriver.

"Sally?" I called, stepping into the room.

There was nobody there. The room was empty.

The last time we couldn't find Sally she'd been in the cherry tree, impossibly high up. She told us Bobby "flied" her there from the open window.

This time the window was closed. I went over and looked out. There was nobody in the tree.

I didn't know whether to be relieved or more scared.

"Well, she has to be somewhere, right?" said Katie, searching the room. She was trying to sound brave but I knew she was as worried as I was.

We looked all over the house, in every room, in all the closets, upstairs and downstairs. No Sally.

"There's only the attic left," I said, opening the narrow door with a feeling of dread. I didn't like the attic.

The attic is where the fear lives.

I jerked my hand away from the door. Where had that thought come from?

"I hear something," said Katie excitedly.

Her voice got through the cobwebs in my head.

Then I heard it, too: scampering feet and a child's laughter.

"Sally!" I hollered, taking the steps two at a time.

I got to the top just in time to see a small foot disappear through the door into the next room.

The attic was broken up into small rooms. Some of them went off at odd angles on account of all the gables. I'd already had one weird experience up here where the little rooms formed a kind of maze and I couldn't find my way out.

"Sally, come back," I shouted.

Katie pushed past me and ran into the next room. But Sally kept going, keeping out of sight, giggling like it was a game.

By the time I caught up with them, I could hear an animal snarling.

It wasn't an animal, it was my little sister. Her eyes burned into us like glowing coals.

"Keep away," she said in a rough, weird voice.

Bobby's voice. A voice from deep in the grave.

My spine tingled. I moved in front of Katie.

"I know it's you, Bobby," I said. "Let me talk to Sally."

"I keep Sally safe," said Sally-Bobby. She pointed at Katie. "Safe from her. Safe from witches!"

The Bobby voice was beginning to sound less

raspy, more like a real kid's voice. For some reason this made my blood run colder.

I inched closer. "Let me talk to my sister right now," I demanded.

"I'm calling your parents," said Katie, turning on her heel. "This is too weird for me. I give up."

As Katie left the room, Sally-Bobby tried to dart around me but I grabbed her and held tight.

She was strong, much stronger than my little sister, but I held on.

Finally she got too tired to struggle. I picked her up and followed Katie downstairs, trying to ignore a few painful kicks in the ribs.

Katie was already on the phone with my parents. "I'm sorry to bother you, Mr. and Mrs. Winter," she was saying, "but Sally's acting very strange and I thought you should know. She's pretending she's some kid named Bobby — a ghost, I guess."

Katie paused to listen. Sunlight fell across her from the kitchen window like a spotlight or a magic circle, leaving me and Sally out in the gloom.

Sally began to struggle in my arms again.

"Bobby is her imaginary playmate?" echoed Katie. "Well, he doesn't seem to like me much. I was wondering, Mrs. Winter, if maybe you could talk to Sally about this Bobby. She's right here."

Katie held out the phone.

"Mommy," cried Sally in her own voice. Her body instantly felt cuddly again instead of hard and tense.

I let her down and she reached eagerly for the phone, the sun catching her blond curls, making them shine like a gold princess crown. "Hi, Mommy!"

Sally listened to the phone for a minute and giggled. "Me and Bobby were just playing," she said. "He doesn't like baby-sitters but I do. I like Katie. We were just teasing." She paused and smiled up at the baby-sitter. "Yes, Mommy, we'll be good. I promise!"

Katie gave me an I-knew-it-all-along look. Now she really believed the haunting was fake!

Just like the house wanted.

17

Dinner wasn't much fun that night, so when I heard a knock on the back door I hoped it was Steve. At least we could hang out in the back-yard together.

But there was nobody there.

"Steve? Are you out there?"

No answer. Just the shadows of night growing longer and longer, and the tree branches sighing in the wind.

I went back to the living room and continued to help Sally put her puzzle together.

Katie was reading, tight-lipped. Still mad at us because she'd been locked in the basement.

A few minutes later she got up and went into the kitchen and a second after that there was a blood-curdling scream.

I ran into the kitchen. Katie stood there shaking, a broken glass at her feet.

"What happened?" I asked.

She pointed at the window. "Something's out

there. It was horrible. This huge hairy face was pressed up at the window, grinning at me."

"What did it look like?" I asked.

Katie shivered. "I don't know. Like a monster, I guess."

"You must have scared it away," I said. "There's nothing there now."

I ran to the door and opened it, which was probably not that smart but there was no one — and no thing — there.

Katie poured another glass of lemonade and we went into the living room.

I was back helping Sally when Katie screamed again.

"No! It's horrible! Horrible!" Katie pointed at the living room window.

I swung around to look just as a hunched shape dropped out of view.

Sally started to cry.

Suddenly something scratched from outside the front door.

"*Katie, I want Katie,*" said a strange, spooky voice through the door. "*I will drink your blood.*"

I yanked open the door and a large lump in a big, black sweatshirt fell into the hall. "Ow!" it cried.

I prodded it with my foot and it got up. Its face was a horrible mass of sores and warts with hairs growing out of them. Blood dripped from one eye.

With a screech of fury, Katie pushed me out of the way and grabbed the thing by the nose.

The horrible face peeled off in her hands.

"Ow," said Steve, rubbing his nose. "Can't you guys take a joke?"

"I've had enough jokes from you two to last me a lifetime," snapped Katie, throwing the mask on the floor and flouncing out of the room.

"You scared my little sister half to death," I told Steve. "You'd better go home."

"Sorry," said Steve. "It was just a joke."

"See you tomorrow," I said. "And no more jokes."

18

Not long after Steve left I went up to my room. The house was a creepy place, no doubt about that, but my bedroom was pretty cool. It was big with high ceilings and a neat, old-fashioned window seat. The kind where you lift a lid that hides a toy box. Not much furniture — just my bed and a battered table I glued airplane models on, and an even rattier old bureau my mom said was a valuable antique.

Built into the closet door was something that was almost as good as a fun house mirror. It made me look like a nine-foot high beanpole with a kink in the middle. If I jumped up and down in front of that mirror it made my reflection slither like a snake.

I messed around with the old mirror for a while, but tonight it was boring. I tried reading, but my books were boring, too. I liked science fiction and scary-monster stuff but somehow with a ghost or two in the house the thrill wasn't the same.

So I put together some warm clothes and rolled up my extra blanket for later. I was going to wait for Katie to go to bed and then go get Sally and take ourselves out to sleep under the cherry tree where, maybe, it was safe. Safer than inside, anyway.

Last night had been no big deal but I didn't think the house would let us off that easy two nights in a row.

And it was my job to keep Sally safe.

So I lay down on the bed with my clothes on and stared up at the ceiling. Trying to stay awake no matter how heavy my eyelids got.

But I couldn't fight it. The bed was so soft. My eyelids drooped and I fell asleep.

The next thing I knew there was a light shining in my eyes.

I was too late. It had started.

My room was filled with silvery blue light. A cold, cold light that made my skin look gray, like a corpse's.

The light was coming out of my closet! No, not the closet. The mirror on the closet door. The mirror was glowing.

A strange, glowing cloud swirled in the center of the mirror.

It was getting thicker, spinning faster and faster. I couldn't stop staring. I tried closing my eyes but I couldn't. It was as if the mirror was hypnotizing me, sucking me in.

The cloud darkened. It was taking shape.

A picture was forming in the mirror!

It was a room. I almost recognized it. Almost — then the cloud dissolved into mist again, swirling and plucking at me.

I sat up, moving like a zombie.

The mist in the mirror came together. It formed the image of a bedroom. A room right here in the house.

My sister must be in danger!

I tried getting up — I wanted to run in and check on her — but suddenly I couldn't move a muscle. I could only stare into the mirror as the picture became clearer and more detailed.

Slowly a bed swam into view, then a long black shape. The shape grew darker and sharper.

It was the old lady, the skeleton thing shrouded in black.

And it wasn't Sally's bedroom, it was Katie's! I recognized her four-poster bed and the flowered wallpaper and could even see a dark blob that must be her head on the pillow.

In the mirror the old witch-thing was bending over Katie.

I watched helplessly as a long bony claw

reached out, sharp bony fingers stretching toward Katie's sleeping head.

Then suddenly there was a popping sound and the mirror flashed and went blank.

My room was plunged into total darkness.

From somewhere in the house came a long, piercing shriek of terror.

"Aaahhhheeeee!"

The scream was cut off.

But the house was not quiet. No, the house wasn't quiet at all.

19

There was a charge in the air. As if the house was getting ready for something big.

Like anything could happen.

Doors creaked. Floorboards moaned. Shadows flitted like tiny bats, just out of sight. There were little whispery noises in the walls, like scratchy fingernails inside the plaster.

Suddenly I could move again.

I wanted to grab my blanket, wake Sally, and get out of here. But first I had to help Katie. I had to.

I could hear her — or someone — thrashing around in her room.

And then another scream ripped the air.

I was out of my room and running down the hall. Running in the dark, my heart pounding in my chest.

I threw open Katie's door.

She had the light on and she was stamping and hopping as if something was biting her ankles. She was tearing at her hair and making high-pitched, yipping noises.

But there was no sign of the old lady ghoul. Just Katie tearing wildly at herself.

"Katie!" I shouted. "What's wrong?"

She whipped her head toward me. Her eyes were rolling with fright.

"Get them out of here," she screamed. "They're in my hair! All over the bed!"

I looked past her at the bed. There was a small box lying open on her pillow. Little brown dots were climbing out of the box and lots more of them were scurrying in every direction, all over Katie's bed and pillow.

I moved a little closer to see what they were.

Spiders! Hundreds of tiny brown spiders. Someone had dumped them all over Katie and her bed. Was it the old witch ghost I'd seen in the mirror?

"Get them out of here!" screamed Katie again, slapping at her ankles and arms and pawing at her head.

I grabbed up the box and started trying to brush the spiders back into it. But there were too many. They kept running out and crawling over my hands and up my arms.

"Kill them!" yelled Katie. She yanked the pillow off the bed and threw it on the floor.

It wasn't the spiders' fault, I thought. But Katie was in no condition to listen to reason.

So I opened her window, took off the screen, and then bundled up her sheets and blanket and threw them out to the grass below.

"The pillow," she insisted, so I tossed that out and then the little box, too, although I didn't think any spiders were left in it.

Then, it couldn't be helped, any spiders that weren't quick enough to scurry into a crack got stomped. Good-bye little bugs, see you in spider heaven.

After I got rid of all the spiders, Katie snatched up a hairbrush and began brushing her hair so hard I thought she'd pull it all out.

"How could you do such a horrible thing?" she demanded, shuddering.

"Me?" I squeaked, totally caught off balance.

"Who else? You're not going to try to blame Sally are you?" Her eyes narrowed. "I suppose you're going to tell me it was Bobby the ghost."

"Well — " I stopped, remembering what I'd seen in the mirror. "Actually, I think it was the old lady ghost. I saw her bending over you while you were sleeping — "

"Whaaat?" Katie's head whipped around so fast I thought she would hurt her neck.

"In my mirror. The one on my closet door. It started to glow and then your room appeared and — "

"That's it!" Katie threw the brush and I ducked just in time. It skittered across the floor and I saw a little brown spider scurry out from under it. "This is the last straw," Katie said. "I'll be calling your parents tomorrow, young man. Until then, get out of my sight!"

I knew it was no use trying to talk to her when she was like that so I checked on Sally, who had slept through the whole thing, and then went back to my room.

I sat on the side of the bed thinking.

Why did the Bobby ghost want to frighten Katie away? She didn't even believe in ghosts, so she was no danger to him. But then again, it wasn't just Bobby who had it in for the baby-sitter: The mirror had shown that it was the old lady ghost who put the box on Katie's pillow.

Were the little boy and the old witch acting together now?

The thought stuck in my chest like a sharp stone.

But what about the image in the mirror? Where had it come from? Somebody had wanted to help Katie.

One thing seemed clear. Ever since Katie arrived, the pressure was off me and Sally. It seemed like Katie was a magnet for all the angry feelings in the house.

What did it all mean? Who exactly was haunting this place and why?

My head was too rattled to think straight. I swung my feet back under the covers.

I reached up my hand to turn off the lamp.

Strange. Because I had never turned the lamp on. So how come the room was filled with light?

I froze, then slowly swiveled my head toward the mirror.

The mirror was glowing again.

The mist swirled in the center and then flew apart. Letters formed. They were faint and shaky, hard to read.

I sat up and concentrated hard.

HELP ME, it said.

Slowly the words faded but the mist returned and more words formed.

SAVE ME.

The wispy letters slowly dissolved, revealing another image deep in the mirror.

I squinted, staring with all my might, and saw what looked like a long, narrow staircase. At the top of the stairs a door swung slowly open.

The attic!

Then the image faded and the room was dark once again.

Shivering, I went back to bed and pulled the covers up to my chin.

I didn't want to go back to the attic. No way.

And how could I save a ghost?

How could anyone help a little boy who was already dead?

20

It was the itching that woke me up.

I sat up scratching, blinking at the daylight that flooded the room.

Itching?

That's when I realized that a couple of the spiders must have bitten me, too. You're not supposed to scratch stuff when it itches, but I couldn't help it.

Which made me think of poor Katie, covered with tiny little spiders. Spiders she thought I'd dumped on her bed.

I jumped out of bed and got dressed quickly. Don't scratch, you moron. But there was an itching in my brain I couldn't ignore: Katie had sworn she was going to call my parents and tell them all the horrible tricks I was playing on her.

Big mistake. That would only make things worse. Something in the house wanted to get rid of Katie, and complaining to my parents wouldn't change that.

Remembering what I had seen in the mirror last night, I felt excited. Bobby had asked for my help! This had never happened before. He had always treated me like the enemy.

But last night something had changed. Even though he didn't like Katie, he sent me a warning in the mirror. That showed he was on our side — against the old witch.

And afterwards he asked for help.

I still didn't know what he wanted, but one thing seemed to make sense. If I could figure out a way to help Bobby, maybe the haunting would stop.

This seemed like such a good idea I wanted to tell Katie about it. Especially before she called my parents.

I hurried downstairs but paused outside the kitchen when I heard Katie's voice speaking to Sally.

"You don't really believe in ghosts, do you?" Katie was saying. "A big girl like you?"

"No," Sally answered solemnly. "Not me."

"And you know that Bobby is just pretend, right? An imaginary friend?"

"He's not imaginary," Sally replied. "He's just invisible."

It seemed like a good moment for me to interrupt. I poked my head around the corner.

"Um, good morning, everybody," I said. I couldn't believe how wimpy it came out. Even though I hadn't done anything, I sounded guilty!

Katie gave me a steely-eyed look. "I've decided not to call your parents," she said abruptly. "I'll give you one more chance."

Turning back to the stove, Katie flipped eggs in the fry pan. "Your mom and dad have important work to do and they're relying on me," she said. "I'm not going to let your infantile sense of humor wreck everything."

She dumped eggs and bacon on a plate and banged them down in front of me.

I made a face. It was so unfair! She was so stubborn and closed-minded about everything.

But I had to convince her. I had to try.

How could she watch out for Sally if she didn't believe in the danger?

"Listen, Katie," I began. "We need to have a serious talk. There are things you should know about what's going on here."

That's when Sally started whimpering and fidgeting and wouldn't stop until Katie picked her up.

At first I thought Sally just wanted the attention. But when she met my eyes she smiled secretly, as if she'd made a fuss just to interrupt me.

For some reason Sally didn't want me warning the baby-sitter about the house — she wanted to keep Katie in the dark.

21

Lucy stopped by after breakfast. She had an oversized T-shirt on over her bathing suit and a beach towel slung over her shoulder. Her dark ponytail was pulled through the back of her baseball cap.

She squinted at me under the brim of the cap. "What's the matter with you? You're looking kind of pale." Her eyes widened. "More ghost stuff?"

I told her about the mirror and how I'd seen the old lady bending over Katie. But when I got to the part about the spiders, Lucy started laughing so hard she fell down holding her stomach.

"Stop it," I said, "or I won't tell you the rest."

"I can't help it," she gasped, clutching her side. "You shooing the spiders out the window and poor Katie with bugs in that beautiful red hair, it's very funny."

"There's more," I said.

Lucy suddenly looked serious. "I should have known," she said.

"When I got back to my room the mirror started glowing again," I said, describing the message and the image of the attic stairs.

Lucy shivered a little even though the sun was hot. "What does it mean?" she asked.

"I guess Bobby thinks I can find something in the attic that will help him. Somehow."

"How do you know it's Bobby?" asked Lucy, squinting at the house intently. "It might be another trick. The house trying to get you into the attic."

I shivered. "Maybe you're right. Whatever, I'm not going up into that attic, no matter what."

"Forget it," Lucy suggested. "What you need is a dip in the lake."

She raced me to the lake and won, but only because I tripped over my Nikes like an idiot and fell flat on my face. I made up for it by outswimming her to the raft and back.

The water was warm and clear and it seemed to make my head clear, too. What was I doing letting bad dream stuff ruin my summer vacation?

The house was haunted, sure, but it hadn't hurt us yet. All it could do was try to scare us away. And a thing can't scare you if you won't let it, right?

Right?

I came back from the lake feeling refreshed. Nothing was going to scare me — not a lot of noises in the night, or spooky laughter in the walls. No way.

"Come on in," I said to Lucy. "I'll ask Katie if you can stay for lunch."

I knew something was wrong as soon as we entered the front hall. The house seemed to suck up sunlight like a black hole. Dust hung in the air, making the place look even more dreary than usual.

"It doesn't look like anyone has changed a thing in this place for a hundred years," Lucy said in a hushed voice. "This house doesn't need a ghost to be creepy."

"Katie!" I called out. "We're home!"

"Sally!" I called out. "Are you here?"

There was no answer.

"What's that?" Lucy whispered.

I listened. At first I didn't hear it. Then it came again.

A moan, from deep inside the walls.

A ghostly moan, like something trapped in a tomb.

22

As we went up the stairs, Lucy grabbed hold of my hand and wouldn't let go.

The moaning noise had stopped but I knew it wasn't over. It was like the old house was holding its breath.

I'd never known that silence could be so loud.

I tensed when we got to Sally's room, expecting the worst. As I pushed the door open the creaking noise from the hinge went through me like a jolt of electricity.

Beside me Lucy gave a little gasp.

"Thank goodness," she said, sighing with relief.

Sally was sound asleep on her bed. She was hugging Winky, her stuffed rabbit.

I gently closed the door. Glad that *somebody* could sleep around here.

"*ARRRGGH.*"

A long, low moan froze us in our tracks.

Lucy went white and her eyes were as big as Oreos.

"It — it's coming from up there," Lucy said, pointing at the ceiling.

She was right. The ghostly moaning was coming from the attic.

"It sounds like somebody is hurt," Lucy whispered.

"Maybe that's what it *wants* us to think," I said.

Lucy got a very determined look on her face. "We've got to check it out," she said.

My mind resisted. But I couldn't let Lucy go alone.

"Okay," I sighed. "Let's get it over with."

When I opened the door to the attic stairway, shadows seemed to spill out, dimming the hallway.

"This is a really bad idea," I said. But I started up the stairway. My Nikes made squeaky noises on the bare wooden steps.

It was hard making myself go up those stairs. It was as if lead diving weights had been attached to my feet, holding me back.

"Uuurrrggg."

The strange sound went right through me.

I turned around to run back down the stairs and bumped into Lucy. I could tell she was just as scared as me.

"What do we do?" she whispered.

The seconds ticked away like blood dripping. I braced for another cry, but the attic stayed quiet.

"Come on," I said, leading the way. "We're acting like boneheads."

I trooped up to the top of the stairs before I could change my mind and barged right through the door into the attic.

Suddenly I was blind. I couldn't see.

I was choking on dust and the sunlight was blasting in like a laser beam. Behind me Lucy was coughing and choking.

The moaning noise came again, louder.

By now it sounded almost familiar. It wasn't coming through the walls, it was right in the room with us. Only we couldn't see because of all the dust in the air.

"Jason, help me. Help me please."

I knew that voice. It wasn't the ghost, it was Katie.

"Over here," she said, sounding weak. "I'm trapped."

I kept squinting and after a while I could see through the dust. A big wooden beam had come crashing down from inside the roof, smashing into the plaster walls.

And under the beam was Katie.

All I could see at first was a pink sandal sticking out from under the beam. It looked really bad. Then I saw her toes wiggle.

"Give me a hand," I said to Lucy.

We both grabbed the end of the beam and managed to shift it over, away from where Katie was trapped.

"Are you okay?"

Katie crawled out from under the wrecked plaster. At first I thought her red hair had turned white — then I realized it was all the plaster dust.

We helped Katie to her feet. She heaved a huge sigh. "Thanks, guys. It feels so good to breathe again. It was awful to hear you calling me and not be able to answer."

"What happened?" I asked. "Are you sure you're okay?"

Katie winced a little and limped away from the wreckage. "Just bruised, I think. I'll tell you about it downstairs. I don't want to spend another second up here."

Lucy and I helped her down the stairs from the attic. She looked pretty weird with all that white stuff in her hair, but for some reason I didn't feel like laughing. That beam that had fallen on her was big and heavy.

She was lucky to be alive.

23

The first thing Katie did when we got downstairs was wash her face in the sink and then get a big glass of water. She drank the whole glassful, sighed, and slumped into a chair at the kitchen table.

"Something very weird happened," she said. "I saw this little boy on the stairs. He had very pale skin and he was about Sally's age. And he was dressed in old-fashioned clothes."

"The ghost!" I exclaimed. "You really saw him?"

Katie frowned, then slowly nodded. "He beckoned to me," she said. "He looked so sad, I wanted to help him. So I followed him down the hall to the attic stairway. It was like he disappeared through the door, but that may have been my eyes playing tricks on me."

"What happened next?" I asked.

"The door opened. Someone called my name from up in the attic. At first I thought it was you, playing tricks again. But it wasn't your voice. Anyhow, I went up into the attic. There was nobody there. At least not that I could see. Then I heard a noise behind me — like someone was standing there out of sight. I whirled around and that's when the roof came crashing down on me."

"It wasn't the whole roof," I said. "Just one beam and part of the ceiling."

"Well, it sure felt like the whole roof. I couldn't move. I tried shouting for you but you didn't hear me."

I said, "We were down at the lake. And Sally was sound asleep. It's a good thing we came back when we did."

Katie nodded and took another drink of water. "It sure is," she said. "But that's not all. When I was pinned under the beam someone came into the room. I could hear the footsteps. And then whoever it was started laughing."

"Laughing?" I said.

"It was horrible," Katie said with a shudder. "Horrible laughter. Cackling, like some old witch."

I jumped up from the table. "That was her! The old witch ghost!"

Katie gave me a strange look. "There was something else," she said. "She smelled terrible."

"What do you mean, terrible?" I asked.

Katie looked at both of us. She took a deep breath and said, "She smelled like she was . . . dead."

24

That night I went to bed with the lights on. Taking no chances. I didn't even bother with pajamas, I just got under the covers with my clothes on.

No way was I going to fall asleep. Bad things happened when you fell asleep in this house.

So I sat up in bed and read a pretty cool sci-fi story, figuring that would keep me awake. And I ate peanut butter crackers, because the crumbs in the sheets would help keep me awake, too.

I don't remember falling asleep, but I must have. Because the next thing I knew the grandfather clock was chiming and I woke up with a start. Every muscle in my body was tense.

And the lights were out. I'd left them on, but now it was pitch black.

The clock.

BONGGGGGG. BONGGGGGG. BONGGGGGG.

In the daytime it was broken. It only came to

87

life at night, when something terrible was about to happen.

I lay rigid as a board, waiting. Waiting.

There wasn't long to wait. It was the same thing I'd heard before.

First a child crying, sounding scared and angry. Calling his mother.

"*Mom-meeeeeeeeeee.*" A child's voice echoing from the grave.

Then the patter of tiny running footsteps. A child running down the hallway outside my door.

And chasing him, heavier footsteps. *Thump-thump-thump.*

I heard the child panting, out of breath.

But still he came running, closer and closer.

It sounded like the panting was in my room. I could hear his frightened breath tearing from his chest — right beside my ear.

I bolted up in bed.

There was no one there. The room was dark and still.

Out in the hall the footsteps kept coming.

They ended in a sharp scream — *aaahhhhhhhhh!* — as the boy went hurtling over the banister.

And there came the sickening thud of a small body hitting the floor.

My heart was pounding.

I lay down and pulled the covers over my head.

The crying would start again soon but I wouldn't get up.

No way. I was staying right here in my bed.

Listening to the little boy's ghost was horrible but it no longer scared me. There was nothing I could do to make it stop. To make it better.

I closed my eyes tight.

Out in the hall a door opened.

"Who's there?" called out a quavery voice.

Oh, no. It was Katie.

But that meant she could hear the ghost! Unlike Mom and Dad who never woke up no matter what happened.

I didn't know if it was good or bad that she could hear it, too.

"Sally? Is that you?" she called out. "Are you all right?"

I wanted to yell at her to go back to bed.

Nothing good ever came of getting up in the night.

"Sally?" Katie's voice was drifting away.

Oh, no! She was going downstairs.

I had to stop her. I whipped off the blankets and started for the door.

I had my hand on the doorknob when I heard the first scream.

25

The hallway was pitch-dark, as usual. The lights never worked on nights the old clock chimed.

Another scream pierced the air.

I hurried toward the stairs, feeling my way along.

A strange light glowed from downstairs. Then something smashed into a wall and glass tinkled over the floor.

Katie cried out and a second later there was the crash of something big falling.

Another shattering sound, another scream.

Furniture turned over and smashed. More glass broke. It was like the living room was turning itself upside down.

I saw a vase lift itself off the shelf of knick-knacks and hurtle down toward Katie at the bottom of the stairs.

"Get down, Katie!" I shouted.

Always before I had been the target. It was weird seeing it from this angle.

Peering around the banister, I could dimly see Katie cowering, dodging, trying to cover her head.

A figurine left the shelf behind me, then a silver tray, and a blue glass candy dish.

I gasped in surprise. From here I could see that none of this artillery was aimed directly at Katie. All the objects were shooting over her head toward something behind her.

"Katie! Keep your head down!" I called out. "Lie flat on the floor!"

Instantly she threw herself down.

And then I could see something behind her — a tall figure, hooded and draped in black. Around the thing the air seemed denser, as if no light could penetrate.

Oddly, this weird effect made the thing more horrible and easier to see at the same time. It was edged in black against the darkness.

It raised one arm. The arm was impossibly long, stretching sticklike to the ceiling.

A bright glint of metal caught my eyes. I gasped out loud.

Was the thing made of steel?

It moved and metal gleamed again.

A silver candlestick! It was holding a heavy candlestick over its head — that was what made the arm appear so long.

The black thing raised its other arm to grasp the candlestick with two hands.

It glided toward Katie, who was lying face down on the floor. It reared back with the candlestick, poised to bash in her skull.

I tried to shout a warning but it was too late. Much too late.

26

The scream tore out of my throat.

Katie's head jerked.

The candlestick flashed in the dim light.

And the bronze baby shoe suddenly flew off the shelf beside me.

The heavy bronze baby shoe struck the shrouded creature with a solid THUNK!

The creature squealed in pain. The candlestick dropped to the floor and the creature vanished into the shadows.

Instantly everything was still.

"Katie? Are you all right?" I asked, running down to her.

"I've never been so terrified," she said, hoarse from screaming. "I thought I was going to be killed."

"We better get upstairs," I said, helping her up. "It might come back."

"What might come back?" she said.

"The thing in the shadows."

Katie didn't say anthing more until we got back to her bedroom door. Then she folded her arms and stared down at me, looking very stern — her baby-sitter look. "What thing in the shadows, Jason? What are you talking about?"

"The old witch ghost," I explained. "That's what Bobby was throwing all the stuff at. He was trying to protect you from the old witch."

Katie shook her head. "Whaaat? I've swallowed a lot, Jason, but that's going too far."

"Look," I said. "I know you don't want to believe me, but there are two ghosts haunting this house. They're fighting over something — I don't know what."

Katie gave me a long look. "Maybe it was you who was throwing all those things."

"You know it wasn't me," I said. "You heard the clock chime and the ghosts running through the hall. That's what woke you up, right?"

"I guess so," she said.

"That's what happened to you up in the attic. The two ghosts were fighting and you got in the way."

Katie rubbed her head. "Maybe. I don't really believe in ghosts, Jason, but just for the sake of argument, let's say you're right. What do you suggest?"

I thought about it. "I suggest you go back to bed, lock your door, and don't come out, no matter what."

27

"I won't sleep now," said Katie. "I'll just grab a blanket and sit up in Sally's room."

That was my plan, too. But no way I could tell Katie I didn't trust her to watch out for Sally. So I went back to bed, pulled the covers over my head, and tried to sleep.

But it was no use. Questions bombarded me from every side.

Why had the haunting become focused on Katie?

Was Bobby an evil spirit trying to take over my little sister Sally and keep her with him forever? Or was he the spirit of a confused and unhappy little boy who had scary temper tantrums? Both, probably.

Why did the old witch want to attack Katie? Why did Bobby, who violently disliked Katie, save her? Was it Bobby who saved her?

These questions bounced around in my mind like crazy rubber balls.

The room began to get light. I'd had no sleep and night was over, the sun was coming up. Maybe it was just as well.

But the light was funny. Too blue to be sunlight. The mirror!

I pulled the covers off my head and, sure enough, my closet mirror was glowing.

The mist formed and out of it came an image: the attic stairs, shrouded in fog.

I felt a tug. The bedclothes began to slip off me.

Yikes! I grabbed the blanket with both hands.

I absolutely positively wasn't going into the attic by myself in the middle of the night. No way, no how.

In the mirror the attic door opened wider. Sparkles danced in the inky blackness. The sparkles grew thicker and gleamier, like a curtain of fairy dust. The curtain parted. A small boy appeared in the doorway, sparkles swirling around him like stars. He was pale and sad, with huge, beseeching eyes.

Then it happened. Something seemed to take control of my body. Like a sleepwalker I got out of bed.

Something made me walk to the door, open it, and go down the dark hallway, toward the attic stairs.

Part of me deep inside was screaming NO! STOP THIS RIGHT NOW! GO BACK TO BED!

But I couldn't resist. My feet kept right on moving.

The door to the attic stairway swung open soundlessly.

I knew that whatever waited on the other side was dark and terrible. But warm light spilled from the stairway out into the hall, beckoning me.

I started up the stairway into the attic. Soft light seemed to shine down from the attic.

Fear was like a small stone lodged in my throat.

My heart was quaking, but some irresistible force made me keep going, climbing to the top.

I stepped into the attic and found myself in a room I had seen once before. A little boy's bedroom decorated from the old days. Bobby's room.

It was bathed in soft yellow light, like sunlight.

A child's rocking chair rocked gently in the corner. There was a small toy chest against the wall.

Bobby wanted me to open it.

I was kneeling in front of the chest, hands reaching for the lid, when the spell broke.

I snapped back to myself, every sense alert.

Something was wrong.

Then I heard it. Stealthy footsteps coming up the attic stairs.

The black-draped witch had followed me!

A floorboard groaned.

The heavy footsteps stopped.

I pressed my ear to the door. The footsteps resumed, creeping quietly closer.

There was only one thing to do. Wait until it got to the top, then whip open the door and shove it down the stairs.

Nails scraped along the door.

The moment had come.

I took a deep breath and yanked open the door.

A shape loomed, rising over me.

Bracing myself, I reached for the thing and pushed.

It grabbed me instead!

Claws sunk into my arm, clutching me in a death grip!

28

I t screamed.

It?

"Jason! What are you doing?"

Katie?

She was starting to fall. What had I done?

I gripped her wrist and pulled. Katie fell forward into the attic.

"I thought you were going to push me down the stairs," she said, giddy with relief.

Why had I been so sure she was the thing in the black cloak?

But there was no time to think about this — the house was starting up again.

The warm light dimmed. The child's chair began rocking crazily.

"Jason, what's happening?" Katie asked, her voice rising.

"Just hang on," I said.

A gale-force wind rushed up the stairs and

began whipping around the walls of the little room. It snatched the breath from my mouth.

Then the wind grabbed Katie and — WHAM! — flung her up against the wall.

"I don't think Bobby wants you here!" I shouted against the wind.

The mysterious wind let up slightly and Katie pried herself from the wall. "I'm staying," she vowed defiantly. "Nothing is going to make me leave. I'm going to help, no matter what!"

Her jaw was clenched with determination, although her eyes darted wildly with fright as the wind slammed her once more against the wall. "No matter what!" she screamed again.

All the wind rushed together to form an angry funnel in the center of the room. It was like a miniature, deadly tornado.

We would both be dashed to pieces in its fury.

The funnel traveled back and forth between us. It sounded like an engine at the highest pitch, ready to explode.

"We want to help!" shouted Katie, her voice cracking with strain.

Suddenly the funnel moved to the old toy chest near the rocking chair. The lid blew back and papers swirled into the air.

And the wind was gone, just like that.

Katie and I stared at each other, catching our breaths.

A scrap of newspaper drifted to settle at my

feet. I bent and picked it up. As I read, excitement stirred in the pit of my stomach.

"Now we know," I said wonderingly.

"Know what?" Katie asked, craning her neck to see over my shoulder.

"Who Bobby was," I said. "And how he died."

29

"**R**obert Wood, killed October 2, 1940, age five."

Katie looked up from the old newspaper with tears in her eyes. "Fifty-five years ago!" she said. "The poor kid has been haunting this house for fifty-five years, waiting for someone to rescue him!"

I snatched the paper from her hand and read on. " 'Robert was killed instantly in a fall from the cherry tree outside his bedroom window. Mr. and Mrs. Herbert Wood, his parents, were on a European trip at the time and Robert had been left in the care of a nanny, Alice Everett.' "

"The poor nanny," said Katie. "How horrible I'd feel if anything happened to you or Sally while your parents were gone."

I shivered. She was right — the situations were pretty similar. Did that mean the time was ripe for another fatal accident?

" 'The nanny,' " I read, " 'was beside herself

with grief and there were signs the balance of her mind had been affected. Miss Everett, twenty years of age, kept repeating that the child's teddy bear was missing. Oddly, this favorite toy had still not been found at the time of the child's burial.' "

Katie shuddered. "I wonder what happened to the poor woman?"

We gathered up the other newspaper clippings that had blown around the floor. They were mostly repeats of the same story. One had a description of the teddy bear — brown with a mended ear.

As I put the clippings away I noticed another piece of paper face down at the bottom of the box.

"What's that?" asked Katie.

It was stuck in a corner of the box and didn't want to come loose. I tugged gently, afraid to rip the old paper. "I think it's a photo," I said. "But I can't see who's in it."

"Here," said Katie, nudging me aside. "Let me try."

Just then the paper came free, slipping easily into my fingers.

"That must be Bobby with his mother," exclaimed Katie when I turned over the photo.

It showed a small boy and a pretty young woman in a wide-brimmed hat, which must have been fashionable at the time.

"They don't look very happy," I said, noticing that both the boy and the woman had pretty grim expressions.

"That was the style then," said Katie knowingly. "People never smiled for the camera. Picture taking was serious business."

It was so sad, looking at the photo of a small boy who would never get any older and his pretty mother who would be so far away when he needed her.

"What's that?" said Katie suddenly.

I heard it, too. Something small and furtive rolling along the floor.

Then we saw it. A piece of chalk skittering over the floorboards.

"That's strange," said Katie, reaching for the chalk.

Before she could touch it the chalk swooped into the air.

It flew over to the wall and began to write. Very slowly, in large, uneven, childlike letters, it spelled out:

SAVE ME

30

SAVE ME.

The childlike letters glowed for a moment and then faded away.

"Look!" said Katie.

I suddenly realized something had changed in the room. The little toy chest and the rocking chair were gone.

Bobby's old bedroom had vanished and we were back in the dusty old attic.

The newspaper clippings were gone, too, but the old photograph remained in Katie's hand.

"How can we save a ghost?" asked Katie. "A ghost is already dead."

"Let's get out of here," I said. "We'll talk about it later."

I didn't want to stay in that creepy attic a second longer.

Downstairs in the hallway Katie studied the photo again. "Such a sweet little boy," she said regretfully. "We must figure out a way to help him."

"Right now all I want to figure out is how to get a night's sleep."

I went into the bedroom and shoved the bureau up against the door.

Try to get in now, I thought. Just try.

The next morning I came downstairs to find Katie pacing in the kitchen.

Sally had already eaten her breakfast and I was ready for pancakes or whatever, but Katie waved her hand and said, "How can you think about food at a time like this?"

"Easy," I said. "I close my eyes and I see a huge plate of flapjacks."

"Help yourself to a bowl of cereal," she suggested. "When you're finished, I'll tell you about my plan."

"Forget the cereal," I said. "What plan?"

Katie stared at me with bright eyes. "The tree," she said. "We'll chop down the tree!"

I slumped into a chair. What was she talking about? Had last night's adventures unhinged her mind?

"That's where he died, right?" she said. "Remember the newspaper clipping? It said Bobby died falling from the cherry tree."

"Yeah," I said. "So?"

"So if we chop it down, maybe that will free his spirit. The house won't be haunted anymore."

I stared at her. There was something about this plan that bothered me but I couldn't put my finger on it.

"Come on," said Katie, urging me on. "Let's do it now."

Reluctantly I agreed to help her. "We'll need a chainsaw," I suggested.

"No way," Katie said. "Too dangerous. Didn't I see a Boy Scout hatchet in your room?"

"You can't chop down a tree with a hatchet," I protested. "It'll take forever."

"We can make a start," Katie insisted. "Show Bobby we're trying."

There was no arguing with her.

I got the hatchet. It felt surprisingly heavy in my hand and got even heavier as I approached the backyard.

Katie was waiting under the cherry tree, holding Sally by the hand. The branches spread high overhead, the leaves green and healthy.

"You wait over there," she said to Sally, leading her away from the tree.

Sally stood there looking at us, solemn and silent, her bunny Winky dangling from her hand.

"I don't know if this is such a good idea," I said, hefting the hatchet. "Bobby seems to like this tree. It's the only outside place that he goes."

"He's drawn to it, of course," said Katie impatiently. "It's only natural since his spirit is trapped here. Perhaps even a small cut will be enough to set him free."

She stepped back briskly and nodded at me. "Go ahead."

With a sigh I raised my arm, aimed at a spot in the old bark and started to swing.

I felt a sharp tug.

"Hey!"

The hatchet jerked out of my hand.

It whirled up in the air like a boomerang, flashing end over end.

And then it came back at us.

The flying hatchet glinted in the sun. The blade was razor sharp — and it was heading right for Katie.

"Look out!" I shouted. "Duck!"

Katie didn't move. It was like she was frozen to the spot.

The hatchet whipped through the air, aiming for the place between her eyes.

It was too late. I couldn't save her.

From a long way off I heard Sally scream.

31

There was nothing anyone could do — she was doomed!

Then, just as the flying hatchet was about to bury itself in Katie's head, it veered sharply to the side.

Now it was headed straight for me — moving with the speed of a bullet!

No time to dodge out of the way.

I couldn't take my eyes off the gleaming blade as it came closer and closer, tumbling end over end.

Then suddenly it vanished.

I felt the whisper of the whirling blade as it passed before my eyes, but it never touched me. It had disappeared into thin air!

I shook my head, dazed — and saw the hatchet buried to the hilt in the ground an inch from my foot.

Sally came running and threw her arms around

me, sobbing. "Leave the tree alone!" she cried. "Don't touch the cherry tree!"

"We won't; don't worry," I said, my voice shaking from the close call.

Katie was still vibrating with fear. When she got her voice back she said, "Bad idea. I was wrong, I admit it."

"Bobby says don't hurt the tree!"

"We won't. Tell him we won't, okay?"

Sally looked up at Katie. "You have to promise," she said.

"Okay," said Katie, raising her voice. "I promise we won't touch your precious tree!"

With Sally urging us on, we left the backyard and returned to the front porch. When Katie's nerves had calmed, she made a pitcher of lemonade and brought the tray out to the porch.

"Whew!" she said, taking a seat. "That was a close call."

I sipped the lemonade and said, "He could have killed us."

Katie nodded. "Could have, but he didn't. The ghost was trying to give us a message. He wants us to save him, right?"

I nodded. "Except we don't know how."

"I've got another idea," said Katie. "You're gonna love it."

"Your last idea wasn't so hot," I pointed out.

"This is better," she said. "Much better."

She reached into her jeans pocket and pulled

out the old photograph. "See this? Bobby and his mother, right?"

"I guess so," I said.

"He showed it to us for a reason," said Katie. "I think I know why. I'll tell you my theory, but first we have to go down into the cellar."

That made me spill the lemonade.

"No way," I said.

Katie made a face and put her hands on her hips. "What are you afraid of?" she demanded.

"Oh, nothing much," I said. "Just dying."

32

Outside it was a bright summer day. You'd never know it down here, in the dark.

In the cellar shadows drank up all the light.

I couldn't believe I was down here again.

My skin crawled with dread but Katie didn't seem to sense anything strange.

"This place could do with a good cleaning," she said as we reached the bottom of the stairs. "I bet it wouldn't take more than a day to clear out all this junk. Put a couple more lights in and your dad could turn it into a really nice workroom."

"We're not staying that long," I said.

"Now where's that box?" she said, pawing through the piles of old junk. "I saw a box of old clothes down here somewhere."

While she was searching I swept my flashlight beam behind the stairs to make sure nothing was lurking.

"I know this will work," Katie was saying. "Why else would Bobby have showed us that picture? If his mother wasn't in Europe she could have saved him from falling, right? So he wants me to dress up as his mother and save him. It's perfectly logical."

This was her big plan, her new idea, and I thought it was totally crazed.

"It's just not logical," I argued. "When we hear him falling at night it's inside the house, not out in the tree."

That stopped her. For about a second.

"Well," she said. "Maybe one of us should stay out under the tree while the other — "

"No!" I interrupted. "We have to stay together. Upstairs. Where we heard him fall."

Katie cocked her head, considering, then nodded. "Okay," she said, rubbing her hands together. "Let's get started."

As she headed for the boxes a long cobweb snagged at her thick red hair but Katie just brushed it away impatiently.

I followed. Something moved at the edge of my vision but when I looked nothing was there. The muscles under my skin began to jump with tension.

How did I let myself get talked into this?

Some Looney Tunes baby-sitter wants to play dress-up and talks me into going back down into a haunted cellar — I had to be as crazy as she was.

"Look! This is it! The very same hat," cried

Katie, pulling the picture out of her pocket to compare.

She was right. The wide-brimmed hat she'd found was the same one the woman had worn in the old photograph.

Katie clapped the dusty old hat on her head and continued rooting around in the boxes.

Meanwhile I jumped at every little creak and rustle.

"Hold that beam steady, will you?" complained Katie. "I can't see when you keep bobbing it around like that."

I concentrated on keeping the flashlight beam steady.

The longer we stayed down here the tighter my nerves stretched. Katie was having the time of her life — she was so sure that her plan would work, nothing could convince her otherwise.

Finally she found a long dark dress that she thought matched the one in the picture. She held it up to see if it would fit.

"Great. Let's get out of here," I said.

A soft, cackling sound came from the dark corner.

"What was that?" said Katie, freezing.

"What did it sound like to you?" I asked as casually as I could.

Katie shrugged. "Pipes gurgling, I guess. Wait! Something moved," she said, and pointed into a dark corner.

I picked up an old shoe and threw it where she pointed.

A terrified mouse scuttled out from under some junk and disappeared.

But it wasn't a mouse I'd heard.

That evil laugh could only belong to the witch. And if she was laughing, then we were in trouble.

33

It was almost midnight in the house on Cherry Street.

The haunting hour.

We were waiting in Katie's room. Sally was sleeping in Katie's bed, where we could keep an eye on her.

Katie sat across from me in a rocking chair, wearing the long black dress and the wide-brimmed hat and a pair of antique shoes.

It gave me a creepy feeling to look at her. She looked exactly like the woman in the photograph. More like a grown-up than a baby-sitter.

I sort of hoped the ghost wouldn't come tonight. Then maybe Katie would change her mind. I couldn't put it into words, but I thought Katie dressing up as Bobby's mother was a really bad idea.

"Jason?"

I'd almost fallen asleep. "Did you hear something?" I asked.

Katie shook her head. "I'm just a little worried," she said. "What if I'm doing the wrong thing?"

"If you feel that way, let's call it off," I suggested eagerly.

But just then the broken grandfather clock began to chime. Bobby was coming.

We'd run out of time.

The haunting began like always. Footsteps in the hall.

The small steps of a frightened little boy.

"We've got to try," Katie whispered, gathering her courage. "We've got to save him."

She took a deep breath, straightened the hat on her head, and opened the door.

As she stepped out into the hallway the lights went out.

The walls began to glow with a faint, ghostly light.

"Give it to me, it's miiiiinnnnnnne!" A raspy voice echoed from the darkness.

It was too dark to make out Katie's face, but I saw her shiver.

I wanted to run out in the hall and pull her back into the room but it was too late.

The footsteps were already running toward us.

"Mine!" screamed the terrible voice. *"It's mine, all mine!"*

Katie hurried to the end of the hallway. The long black dress made rustling noises.

If I didn't know better, I'd think it was the woman from the photograph.

Katie stood with her arms outstretched at the spot where we heard Bobby go over the banister, night after night.

She became a ghostly shadow in the darkness.

The child's footsteps came faster, faster than any little kid could run.

"*Help!*" screamed a child's voice. "*Help me pleeeeeeeeease!*"

And then came the heavy tread of the pursuer, *boom-boom-boom*.

It all seemed to take so long. It was like time stood still. As if the scared little boy was running and running and not getting anywhere.

But now he was close. Almost here.

I tensed. In another few seconds it would all be over.

Closer, closer.

Suddenly a piercing scream shattered the air. It was like no scream I'd ever heard before.

It was a scream of pure terror, much worse than the desperate cry we always heard when the child went over the banister.

The sound pierced my heart like a knife.

I felt something brush past me like the wind. It almost knocked me off my feet as it hurtled toward Katie.

She crouched with outstretched arms, wanting to save a ghost she couldn't see.

Then something smashed into her!

The force of the blow threw her up off her feet, against the banister rail.

For an instant she seemed to hang in the air. Then she fell.

I ran to the railing, bracing myself for the sound of her body hitting the floor.

Cackling laughter filled the air.

34

I leaned over the railing, expecting to see Katie falling to the floor.

The witch-thing stared up at me, inches from my face.

A white claw grabbed at me but I jumped back. "Jason! Help!"

It was Katie's voice. What I'd thought was the witch-thing was Katie, dangling over the stair banister, high above the floor. Her long dress had caught on the top of the banister.

As all this shot through my fevered brain, I heard the dress rip.

I sprang forward and grabbed her just as the old material gave way.

With the last of my strength I pulled her back over the banister and we both collapsed on the floor.

"What happened?" said Katie, dazed and shivering.

Before I could answer there was a CRACK! of

lightning. In the flash I could see Katie's terror-stricken face.

Thunder rolled over the house, shaking it to the core.

We huddled on the floor as a violent wind battered the house. Somewhere downstairs a window broke.

The wind shrieked — suddenly every window in the house shattered with a huge explosive crash.

The wind invaded the house, howling from every direction, gathering force as it rushed up toward us.

"Sally!" I shouted. "We've got to get to my sister!"

The wind tore the sound out of my mouth, but Katie nodded. She understood.

Gripping one another, we pushed down the hall, fighting the wind every step of the way.

We managed to get back to the bedroom.

Inside, Sally was clinging to the bedpost with one hand, her hair streaming out behind her. With her other arm she clutched Winky.

"Hang on!" I screamed.

Poor Sally was crying and frightened but didn't seem hurt. Our feet crunched broken glass as we ran to her.

As I gathered her up she cried, "Bobby's scared!"

I felt a leap of hope. "Is there anything we can do to help?" I asked.

"No," Sally said, sniffling. "The witch-thing is too strong. She's come back to get him." She buried her head on my shoulder and sobbed.

"We've got to get out of this house!" shouted Katie.

Sure, if the house would let us go.

We kept to the wall in the hallway, pressing our backs against it as we inched along, the wind batting us around like cat toys.

When we reached the stairway we threw ourselves against the banister and held on.

Slowly we pulled our way down the stairs, gripping the railing.

I could see the front door! We were almost there.

At the bottom of the stairs we held tight to one another and inched across the hallway. Under the roar of the wind I heard the echo of evil laughter.

I refused to listen. We were going to make it.

We reached the front door and Katie grasped the doorknob.

She turned the knob and pulled.

The door opened.

Outside it was a beautiful starlit night without even a puff of breeze.

As I lifted my foot to cross the threshold, I felt the house sigh.

And then we were hurtling backwards, sucked up the stairs.

The house had breathed us in again!

The front door banged shut — SLAM.

The wind was too powerful to resist.

Our feet never touched the floor.

The brim of Katie's hat flapped in my face and her dress flew up to blind us. Sputtering, I pushed it off my face, fighting off the smell of the grave.

As we were blown upstairs the attic door opened with a BANG! so hard the doorknob smashed through the wall.

The wind dragged us up the stairs and tossed us into the attic.

It was Bobby's attic. In the corner was the child's rocking chair. No other furniture, not even the toy chest.

The wind stopped abruptly.

As we started to breathe again the attic door slammed shut behind us. We were locked inside.

What did the ghost want with us? Why had the house dragged us back inside?

Before I could figure anything out there was another sharp CRACK! of lightning that made us jump.

Katie screamed.

In the flare of light we saw a tall, hooded figure raising a sledgehammer, ready to strike.

35

We were trapped!

I shoved Sally behind me and pressed against the wall. I could hear the creature coming closer but it was too dark to see clearly.

Somehow, though, I was sure that darkness was no problem for this creature, the witch-thing that finally had us cornered.

There was nothing up here to use as a weapon.

"Get away!" I shouted. "Leave us alone!"

I kicked out with my foot but knew it was no use, I couldn't even see where I was aiming.

Then suddenly a dim, cool light sprang up behind us. It was like the soft, bluish light that came from my closet mirror.

Now I could see clearly — and what I saw was the witch-thing standing right directly in front of me! The evil red eyes glowed inside the black hood.

Then it smiled, revealing hideous teeth.

The sledgehammer came down — SMASH!

I dodged out of the way and the hammer crashed into the floor right where I'd been, putting a jagged hole in the floor.

"Die, Jason! Diiiiiiieeeeee!"

The creature threw back its head and howled with rage. The hood fell back and for the first time I could really see its horrible face.

It looked a thousand years old, a wrinkled white mass like crumpled paper.

The face of an ancient witch with tiny, glittery eyes. Not a skeleton at all. Worse. Much worse.

She shrieked again and fixed me with those evil eyes. I felt like a bug pinned to the wall.

Raising the sledgehammer, she lunged at me.

There was no room to get out of the way.

I ducked and she came at me again.

I slipped. I was sprawled on the floor with the witch-thing looming over me.

There were no second chances.

She threw back her head and let out a shriek of triumph. I felt her foul, garbage breath and saw her stumps of rotted teeth.

"I've got you now, you wretched boy!"

She swung the sledgehammer right at my head.

36

I rolled sideways and the hammer missed by inches.

The witch-thing just laughed that evil laugh.

"Leave him alone!" Katie screamed. In her old-timey get-up she almost looked like a ghost herself.

"Don't touch my brother!" shouted Sally.

But the witch-thing ignored them and raised the hammer again, ready to squash me like a bug.

I was finished.

And then what would happen to Sally? Or Katie? They'd never get out of this alive.

I had to fight even if it was no use.

I tensed my shoulders. When the witch-thing swung at me, I would try to catch the hammer.

I got ready, ignoring the sinking feeling in my stomach.

The creature's glittering eyes bored right through me. She raised the hammer higher, poised to strike.

And suddenly the rocking chair rocketed up out of the corner into the air!

It slammed the old witch in the head, almost knocking her off her feet!

She howled and smashed the chair to bits with her hammer.

Instantly the pieces came together and in seconds the chair rebuilt itself.

The witch-thing hissed with fury and began slugging the walls with her hammer, screaming, *"Give me the jewel, you nasty little boy! It's mine, give it to me!"*

Splinters flew, and larger pieces, too. The witch-thing was so busy raging, it was like she'd forgotten all about us.

It was someone else she was screaming at. Bobby?

"What jewel?" Katie whispered hoarsely. "What's she talking about?"

"I don't know," I said, flinching as spit flew from the creature's ugly mouth. "But you better duck!"

Our voices had reminded the witch-thing of our presence.

Teeth bared in a snarl, she threw the hammer.

Katie tried to twist out of the way but the torn old dress hampered her movements.

The heavy weapon caught her square on the shoulder.

Katie cried out and clutched her arm.

Sally began to cry.

"It's okay, Sally," said Katie between clenched teeth. "I'm all right."

But she wasn't. I could see how her injured arm dangled uselessly. Just like mine had that time I'd broken it riding my bike down Dead Man's Hill.

It was all up to me now.

I had to get both Katie and Sally past the witch-thing and out of here. Somehow.

The hammer had fallen to the floor between me and the creature.

Seeing my one chance, I lunged for it.

So did the witch-thing. She shrieked, spewing foam at the corners of her mouth, and snatched at the handle.

But at the last instant, the hammer whirled around and lashed at her head.

The witch ducked out of the way and screamed. *"You can't stop me! I'll get you, you brat! I'll get you good, you'll see."*

The hammer dropped heavily to the floor and she quickly seized it, cackling in triumph.

The witch-thing had her eyes fixed on my little sister. A lump of a tongue came out and licked her scabby lips as she grinned at Sally.

It was the most evil smile I'd ever seen. It made the hairs prickle on the back of my neck.

"Come here, little girl," she crooned, raising the hammer over her head once more. Sally whimpered.

Katie pointed behind the witch. "Look!" she cried.

The witch-thing cackled as if she'd heard that trick before.

But behind her a window had formed out of blank wall.

We watched in amazement as a lovely yellow moon appeared in the new window.

Then, in a violent explosion, the window blew in!

A powerful tunnel of wind grabbed the black-draped witch and flung her against the wall.

It pinned her there, spitting and sputtering, unable to move.

"Hurry," I shouted, knowing the window might disappear any second. "We've got to get out on the roof!"

I pushed Katie and Sally in front of me toward the smashed-in window.

And braced myself for the wind that would suck us back into the nightmare.

37

But this time the wind didn't try to stop us. The broken window frame slid open as we approached.

I crawled through it to the roof and pulled Sally out after me.

Katie tried to follow, but she snagged her dress.

"Pull hard!" I shouted to Sally.

She helped and we both yanked on Katie's shoulders, trying to pull her out to the roof. But it was no use — Katie was stuck in the window.

"Let me go!" she shouted. "Save yourselves!"

It was the bravest thing I'd ever heard, but we couldn't run away, not when Katie was in danger.

Behind her I heard the witch-thing screaming again.

Then Katie shrieked. "She's got my feet!"

The witch was pulling her from the other side.

I started to lose my grip and Katie inched back through the window. "Run!" she cried. "Get away!"

"Give me your hand!" I shouted.

I grabbed her good hand and held on with all my might. It was like the witch-thing wanted to rip her in two!

I set my feet against the outside of the window and held on. Slowly Katie came back through the window. She groaned in pain when her broken arm bumped against the roof.

Behind her the witch-thing was spitting and snarling.

Suddenly the witch screamed and let go. Poor Katie came shooting through the broken window and smacked her head against the roof.

She was out cold.

"I'll get you!" screamed the witch.

She was coming at us, charging for the window.

"Bobby!" Sally shouted. "Help us please!"

The witch was reaching for us when suddenly the window disappeared.

"Nooooo," came a horrible wail from inside. *"I want them. They're mine! Mine!"*

Sally and I huddled on the roof with Katie's limp body held up between us.

Inside, the witch-thing was back to smashing the walls.

"Bobby won't let her get us," said Sally. "Bobby

doesn't like baby-sitters, but he's sorry about what happened to Katie."

Right, I thought. Katie had tried really hard to save Bobby.

And look where it got her.

38

Somehow I had to get us down from here.
We were on a gently sloping section of the roof.

Cautiously I crept down to the edge to try and see where we were. Bobby had a way of getting the house turned around when he made rooms appear.

We were over the cherry tree.

My heart gave the smallest leap of hope.

The tree was too far away to reach and even if I could reach it from here the branches were too thin to support me.

But if I could shinny partway down the drainpipe, there was a large branch I might be able to grab hold of.

I went back and told Sally what I was going to do. Katie was still unconscious.

"I'll holler to you when I reach the bottom," I told her. "Then I'm going to go in the house and get to the phone. Katie needs an ambulance."

Sally's eyes were big and frightened. "I'm scared," she said.

"I know, but you have to be brave a little longer," I told her.

There were some vines growing up the drainpipe, so the first part was easy. I just hooked my feet around the vines, clutched the top with both hands, and let myself down easy.

Then the vines broke.

I slipped, skinning my hands, but managed to get a grip with my knees and feet.

I looked up. Already the roof seemed a long ways away.

I let myself down a little more. And a little more.

The drainpipe creaked and complained. It was old and brittle and pieces of it flaked off as I made my way down.

I twisted my neck to see where the tree branch was. I was close.

But it looked a lot farther away from the house here than it had from the roof.

No way I was going to be able to reach it.

I'd have to try and slide down the drainpipe the whole way.

My shoulders and arms were already burning with the effort and I couldn't even feel my knees any more.

I looked down. The ground was very far away.

But it was too late to get back to the roof.

If only there was someplace I could rest for a few minutes! Just long enough to get the feeling back in my arms and legs.

Above me there was a sharp CRACK!

The drainpipe jolted and I lost my grip.

I dug in my heels and grabbed the pipe again, pain shooting through my hands as I slipped.

The pipe was shaking! It was trying to throw me off!

One foot slid off into thin air.

I was falling!

39

I struggled to hold on but my hands were slipping.

My whole body was swinging and I couldn't get my foot back on the pipe.

Then my other heel hit something hard. The pipe shuddered. I came to a stop.

For a second I just held on, trying to get my breath. My heart was pounding.

I looked down. My foot had caught on one of the brackets that held the pipe to the house.

Above me there was another CRACK! and a POP!

Something small and heavy smacked the top of my head, hard.

It fell into a fold of my shirt and I could see it was a bolt.

I looked up in horror.

The brackets that held the pipe to the house were giving way under my weight.

Slowly the pipe sagged away from the house. With every groan my section pulled farther from the wall. I could do nothing. Just watch it happen.

Then, with a final loud POP! the whole thing gave way at once and I was sailing through the air, headed for the ground with the pipe still clutched to my chest.

I was falling faster and faster!

Maybe I would only break a leg. That was the best I could hope for.

Then all of a sudden I wasn't falling anymore.

I wasn't on the ground either.

I was suspended in midair, high over the backyard.

Very carefully, I turned my head to look.

The outer branches of the cherry tree had snagged the pipe. Its weight was resting on one of the thickest branches. I could almost reach out and touch the branch from where I was.

A few more inches, if I could only work my way along the pipe that far. A few more inches and I would almost be safe.

Cautiously I worked my way along the pipe to the tree, holding my breath as the pipe dipped and groaned.

I grabbed the branch and swung my leg over. The branch swayed and held me. As I let go of the pipe it snapped and crashed to the ground.

Shuddering, I inched my way up the branch to

the thick trunk of the cherry tree. Hugging the tree, I started down. The branches seemed to come up to meet my feet.

In no time I was on the ground.

I was shaking so hard my legs wouldn't hold me. I tried to shout to Sally to let her know I was all right but all that came out of my mouth was a croak.

Once I got my breath back, though, it was time to go on. I reminded myself this was the easy part.

I still had to go back inside the house. And the witch-thing was waiting for me.

40

Dark clouds moved across the moon, casting huge shadows on the house.

I walked up to the front door. It felt as if my insides were shrinking away from my skin.

What would happen when I opened the door?

Would the wind drag me back up into the attic? Even from the porch I could still hear banging and shrieking going on up there.

The rest of the house seemed quiet.

As if it was just waiting for me to open that door so it could swallow me whole.

But I had to. Katie needed an ambulance. If she didn't get one . . .

I shuddered. I couldn't think about that.

The front door *creeeeeaked* open when I pushed it.

I stepped into the dark hallway. Nothing stirred down here. But from upstairs came the thump of a hammer smashing the walls.

The witch-thing was still going nuts up there.

As quietly as possible I tiptoed toward the phone, wincing at the noise my sneakers made on the broken glass. If the witch heard me I didn't think my chances of getting out were very good.

But she was making so much noise I didn't need to worry.

I brushed glass off the phone and picked it up, punching 911 in the dark.

"Send an ambulance to the big old house on Cherry Street," I whispered. "It's an emergency."

Then I hung up and got out of there fast.

I needed to get back to Sally and Katie.

I remembered there was a ladder in the garage. There was also a ton of junk. Without a light I had to pick my way back to where the ladder was.

With the help of the moon I managed to find it okay but I still had to get it out of there. It was too heavy for me and I kept falling over old tools and broken outdoor furniture.

I was panting with exhaustion by the time I had it free. As I paused to rest, I saw whirling lights coming up the road.

The ambulance.

We were safe.

The ambulance team took over. They set the ladder up and got Katie and Sally down from the roof.

Katie was still unconscious, but breathing.

"How did this happen?" one of the medical people asked me.

I knew they wouldn't believe me about the haunted house, so I didn't even try. "My little sister got trapped out on the roof," I said, making up a story. "Katie tried to rescue her."

At least half of it was true.

"She'll be okay," the ambulance driver said. "But she'll have to spend a few days in the hospital, getting X rays and a cast put on her broken arm."

I sighed with relief and hugged Sally, who hadn't said a word since she came down from the roof. The noise inside had stopped the moment the ambulance arrived.

"Where are your parents?" somebody asked.

"I'm going to call them right now," I promised.

The ambulance driver ruffled my hair. "You did good," he said, "but now we'd better get her to the hospital."

And that was it. They drove away, lights flashing.

Sally and I were alone.

"Poor Katie," Sally said, wiping a tear from her eye. "Bobby is sorry."

I looked back at the house. It seemed to be watching me. I'd promised to call my parents but something told me not to go back inside the house.

Not again. Not at night.

So my little sister and I huddled under the cherry tree until the first streaks of light showed in the sky.

Sally had finally fallen asleep. It was time to make the phone call, but I didn't want to wake her.

And I knew she'd be safe under the cherry tree.

That's my excuse. That's why I went back to the house by myself. How long could it take, making a phone call?

Inside, the house was silent. Not a sound. That made me uneasy.

Where was the witch-thing? Had she faded away when the sun came up?

But I couldn't worry about that, I had to act fast. I went to the kitchen and looked up at the list of numbers Mom had tacked to the wall for Katie.

It wasn't there.

The paper was gone.

It was the only place Mom and Dad's number was written down. I had no idea how to reach them.

Sally and I were alone. Really alone.

Don't miss
THE HOUSE ON CHERRY STREET
Book 3:

The Final Nightmare

I was breathing hard but there was no time to rest. I grabbed the handle of the trunk.

It was lighter than I expected.

But what had I thought was in it? A body?

I heaved and hauled the trunk through the path I'd sort of made, banging boxes and knocking things over.

Then I was clear of the mess of junk and halfway to the stairs. The bottom of the trunk scraped over the dirt floor as I dragged it, my breathsounding ragged in my ears.

I reached the stairs and started humping it up, making an awful racket.

My heart was ready to burst with effort.

Suddenly a black shape darted out of the darkness and rushed me.

The witch was back. Hissing and spitting, she grabbed hold of the handle on the other end of the trunk.

"Mine!" she moaned. *"Mine!"*

I yanked back harder but I was nearly out of strength.

She pulled the trunk down a step, then another, dragging me down, too.

The witch had won again — but I couldn't let go.

My hand seemed permanently frozen to that handle. She was pulling my arm right out of its socket!

Gritting my teeth against the pain, I started to imagine all the horrible things the creature would do to me when she got me back down into the basement.

"The trunk is mine!" she hissed. *"And so are you!"*

Point Horror

Are you hooked on horror? Thrilled by fear? Then these are the books for you. A powerful series of horror fiction designed to keep you quaking in your shoes.

The Claw
Carmen Adams

The Cemetery
D.E. Athkins

The Dead Game
Mother's Helper
A. Bates

The Surfer
Linda Cargill

Caroline B. Cooney Collection
The Cheerleader
The Return of the Vampire
The Vampire's Promise
Freeze Tag
Night School
The Perfume
The Stranger
Twins
Caroline B. Cooney

April Fools
Help Wanted
The Lifeguard
The Mall
Teacher's Pet
Trick or Treat
Richie Tankersley Cusick

Camp Fear
My Secret Admirer
Silent Witness
The Body
The Window
Carol Ellis

Vampire's Love 1: Blood Curse
Vampire's Love 2: Blood Spell
Janice Harrell

Funhouse
The Accident
The Invitation
The Fever
The Train
Diane Hoh

Driver's Dead
The Yearbook
Peter Lerangis

The Watcher
Lael Littke

The Forbidden Game:
The Hunter
The Chase
The Kill
L.J. Smith

Amnesia
Dream Date
The Boy Next Door
The Diary
The Waitress
Sinclair Smith

The Mummy
The Phantom
Barbara Steiner

Point Horror

Beach House
Beach Party
The Baby-sitter
The Baby-sitter II
The Baby-sitter III
The Baby-sitter IV
The Boyfriend
Call Waiting
The Dead Girlfriend
The Girlfriend
Halloween Night
The Hitchhiker
Hit and Run
R.L. Stine Collection
The Snowman
The Witness
R.L. Stine

Thirteen Tales of Horror
Thirteen More Tales of Horror
Thirteen Again
Various

The R.L. Stine Special Edition
The Diane Hoh Special Edition
The Caroline B. Cooney Special Edition

Unleashed
Transformer
Philip Gross

Blood Sinister
Celia Rees

Point Rmance

If you like Point Horror, you'll love Point Romance!

Anyone can hear the language of love.

Are you burning with passion and aching with desire? Then these are the books for you! Point Romance brings you passion, romance, heartache, . . . and *love*.

Encounter worlds where men and women make hazardous voyages
through space; where time travel is a reality and the fifth dimension a
possibility; where the ultimate horror has already happened and
mankind breaks through the barrier of technology...

The Year of the Phial
Joe Boyle

Virus
Molly Brown

The Obernewtyn Chronicles:
Book 1: Obernewtyn
Book 2: The Farseekers
Isobelle Carmody

Scatterlings
Isobelle Carmody

Skitzo
Graham Marks

Strange Invaders
Stan Nicholls

Random Factor
Human Factor
Jessica Palmer

First Contact
Nigel Robinson

Strange Orbit
Margaret Simpson

Siren Song
Sue Welford

Read Point SF and enter a new dimension...

POINT FANTASY

Read Point Fantasy and escape into the realms of the imagination.

Doom Sword
Peter Beere
Adam discovers the Doom Sword and has to face a perilous quest...

Brog the Stoop
Joe Boyle
Can Brog restore the Source of Light to Drabwurld?

Book of Shadows
Stan Nicholls
Magic so terrible as to be beyond imagining...

The Renegades Series:
Book 1: Healer's Quest
Book 2: Fire Wars
Book 3: The Return of the Wizard
Jessica Palmer
Journey with Zelia and Ares as they combine their magical powers to battle against evil and restore order to their land...

Realms of the Gods
Tamora Pierce
The barrier's gone ... and no one's in control...

Elfgift
Elfking
Susan Price
The cry went out for vengeance...